A Lasting Harmony

A Lasting Harmony

A Thurston Hotel Novel
Book Five

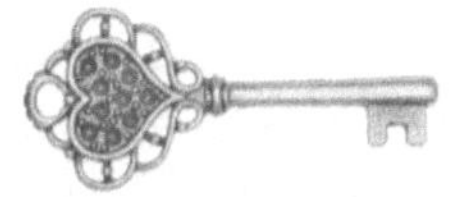

BY SHELLEY KASSIAN

Published 2018, 2016 by Shelley Kassian (shelleykassian.com)

ISBN: 978-0-9948385-8-2 (Print edition)
ISBN: 978-0-9948385-6-8 (Kindle edition)
ISBN: 978-0-9948385-7-5 (Other digital edition)

Design and cover art by Su Kopil, Earthly Charms
Copyediting by Ted Williams

DEDICATION

For Shelley Patty,
A young girl,
who stood at the screen-door of her life
and sang to the world:
I go out walking, after midnight…
I wonder what the neighbors thought.

PREFACE

A Lasting Harmony is book five in The Thurston Hotel series. The novel was written in collaboration with ten Alberta authors and was first published on October 27, 2016.

The fictional Thurston Hotel with its majestic sandstone facade was imagined in the fictional town of Harmony. A welcoming community where the Thurston family, residents, interesting travelers, and even a ghost call the hotel home. While the twelve novels in the series are stand-alone books, each story incorporates Riley Hamilton, a bride preparing for her December wedding.

This novel was my first experience in imagineering a book series with other authors. It's challenging plotting and structuring your own story. Drafting an imaginary hotel with various design details came with authorial challenges. The authors had different ideas and opinions of how the hotel should appear. The team eventually settled on a design that resembled Calgary's Fairmont Palliser Hotel in grandeur and appearance. And then came the town of Harmony's planning phase of character housing, town stores, hospital, fire department, schools, retirement homes, and anything else each author might require for their stories. We were quite the planning crew, imagineering details that sometimes caused stress but more often than not shouldered surprise. I'm proud of the success the series has become. And then there's my story… *A Lasting Harmony*.

Jade Carter, a country and Western singer, struggles with addiction. She arrives at the hotel during the month of May. Her love interest is a bartender? Quite a conflict when a girl has an issue with alcoholism.

In the midst of writing this novel, the town of Fort McMurray faced a forest fire, forcing the largest evacuation in Alberta's history. Given this story was set in the Rocky Mountains of Alberta, Canada, it seemed appropriate to incorporate the fire into my plot.

I hope you enjoy reading *A Lasting Harmony*, and the other titles in the series, too.

Shelley Kassian

ACKNOWLEDGMENTS

The Thurston Hotel novels and this story could not have been written without the imagineering and guidance from Brenda Sinclair and Suzanne Stengl. I thank my colleagues for their conception of The Thurston Hotel novels and in particular, their editorial feedback for *A Lasting Harmony*.

I also thank Katie O'Connor for writing meetings and friendly support when my personal goals conflicted with writing this story. I can see now that when we persevere and believe in ourselves, we can accomplish more than we thought possible!

The story is set in the fictional town of Harmony, but eleven authors chose a real location to assist in the visioning process. Canmore is nestled in the Rocky Mountains of Alberta, Canada. One afternoon, Brenda and I sat writing our novels while gazing at The Three Sisters mountain peaks, a time of year when summer still offered a warm breeze. If you're ever in the vicinity, take a walk along Main Street. You'll feel like you're in Harmony.

CHAPTER 1

Jade Carter suspected her music career was about to grind to a screeching halt. Dixon Reed's phone call and subsequent news had taken her by surprise. She tried to understand what an unscheduled meeting might imply, as the brief conversation with no preamble and a curt tone of voice had left her rattled and upset.

Important news, we must meet in person…

Now that she sat in front of her agent's desk, waiting for him to speak, she scrutinized his expression and acknowledged his beaten look. He was too contemplative, and too quiet.

Normally an animated man, she'd never seen him so somber. *What was he holding back?* Dixon opened his mouth, drew a deep breath, and…

"The Agency has released you from your contract."

The absolute worst news of her career. "No…" Jade bellowed, crying aloud. She rose from the lounge chair, clutched her head in her hands and stumbled backward. The office walls seemed to press in from every side and the air felt stale and bereft of oxygen. She couldn't breathe, could scarcely draw a breath of air inside her lungs.

"What did you say?" She inhaled, trembling.

"I'm sorry," Dixon asserted, his tone forceful. "I wish I didn't have to say this again, but the Agency has released you from your contract."

Frustrated, she crossed her arms and wandered to the heritage windows, soon gazing through thick panes of glass. "Why?" she probed, watching the rain spill from gray clouds to West Hastings Street, seven floors below.

"Look, I knew this news would be hard for you to face…"

Jade threw up her hands, not wanting to hear his excuses. *The gig was up.* She already grieved the loss of her music career and the songs that would never be sung. She might never tour the home of country music again. Nashville—the Grand Ole Opry—a country music stage and a circular swath of wood; with this *finale*, she'd never stand on its history again. The pain was too much to bear.

"Why are you doing this to me?" She appealed, facing Dixon.

"It's a business decision and nothing more. The Agency cares about your well being, cares about your health, too. But with the impossibility of performance, the negative publicity and the lack of engagements, maintaining our agency agreement is impossible. We must release you from your contract."

"I can't believe this is happening," Jade said, taking a deep quivering breath. Her fingers twitched; she couldn't control the movement. She longed for a cigarette to massage between them, or something stronger and more liquid to hold. "I am nothing without my career. I can change, Dixon. I can beat this habit."

Sighing, he rose from his black leather chair and walked

toward her from a sleek mahogany desk. "You can overcome your addiction, if you want to."

"Do you think I haven't tried?" she shouted, meeting his somber expression. "I've been at a rehabilitation center for the last three months, learning how to do just that."

"Let's not belabor the point. We've been down this road before." Approaching her, he touched her arm, but she brushed off his contact. "Your substance abuse has changed you," he warned, stepping away. "Transformed you into a bitter and spiteful woman. The ugly truth is this: the Agency can't market a singer who cannot maintain her commitments."

"But, I've attended every single performance."

"Sure, but you have a bad habit of arriving late for the show, and while on stage, you force the audience to suffer through terrible rants, bouts of moodiness, bad temper and ill-focus. Disappointing your fans is not keeping your commitments."

"Thanks for labeling it so clearly for me."

"Even now, you don't understand," Dixon ground out, appealing to her with both hands. "You need to hear what I have to say. You're a drunk! A woman consumed with drugs and alcohol. The audience pays to hear you sing. No one wants to listen to drunken stories about your life. I'm saying this for your own good. Listen to me! Pull yourself together. Save yourself before it's too late."

Jade had to be dreaming, or having a nightmare. Dazed, she slid her fingers through her hair. She glanced at her palm and reflected on the ginger strands that pulled free from her scalp. Shame caused her to stare downward, unable to face her former agent's nut-brown eyes.

"I've been released from rehab, Dixon. I'm clean right now. I can beat the addiction. I'm trying; I'm fighting the cravings with everything that's in me. I can…"

She saw where his attention wandered, to the bright red strands that lay against her fingers. "Take this pause in your career to get well. Go away. Take a vacation. Heal whatever demons that are encouraging your downfall."

"With what paycheck?" she lamented, tears slipping from her eyes. "I'm a star…" Her voice broke. "I'll die without my fans."

"Jade Carter—" He grabbed her shoulders, shaking her roughly, staring earnestly at her eyes. "If you don't recognize the cost of your addiction, you'll pay a much higher price than losing an agency contract. You'll die." He paused then, as if searching for wiser words. "Leaving your body for some poor young maid to find. I've seen stars succumb to death before, and I know, I'll witness their demise again."

He grasped her hand. "I care about you," he declared, squeezing her fingers. "More than you realize. I want to see you get well, not slip into an early grave."

Jade's voice broke; she earnestly began to cry. "Please… Give me another chance." She sobbed, begging. "I can change. I can. I promise, I won't let you down again."

Dixon released her hand. "I tell you what," he sighed, stepping away. "I see your hands shaking. I know the hell you're fighting through. I'll make you a promise. It's a risk, but I've taken risks before. If you're still clean in say, six months' time— we'll talk, we'll consider a new contract."

Jade contemplated Dixon's earnest expression, grateful for a second chance and hoping he might keep his promise. "I can do it. I promise you I can."

"And let me tell you," he exclaimed, pointing his finger. "I'll know if you've fallen off the wagon. Liabilities show up in abundance on TMZ. If I see so much as a high-shriek giggle on that show, a ramble of speech impediment to anyone in the media, or even a high definition photo from the paparazzi, the offer is off the table. Don't even waste my time by showing up here again."

Jade swallowed a breath. "I promise," she retorted, hoping she'd be able to keep her word. "I won't disappoint you this time."

"Don't disappoint yourself, bestselling country music artist. This situation is not so much about an Agency as it is about a woman named Jade Carter."

She nodded, not knowing what else to say. She supposed they had reached the end.

"Good bye, Dixon. I'll see you in six months' time."

Jade fled from his workspace, not waiting to hear his response. She walked along a corridor of office spaces that were partitioned with expensive etched glass, in no hurry to reach the front reception area. She reached for a Kleenex from the box on Patty's desk and dabbed the soft tissue against the corners of her eyes.

"I have a package for you," Patty stated with an uncomfortable calm. "I'm sorry. I have a final remittance, and I do apologize that the sum is small. There's also some mail, which I presume is from your fans."

Jade watched Patty rise from her swivel chair to collect a yellow manila envelope. "If I still have fans, Patty."

"There's something else."

"What more could there be?"

"The penthouse suite," Patty said with a grimace, leaning against her desk. "You'll need to vacate it within sixty days.

Dixon wanted to give you enough time to find a new place to live."

The news came as a shock; Jade didn't know how to respond. She swallowed, placing her fingertips on her lips. "That's not much time."

"It's the best we could do." Patty passed the envelope over a white enamel counter.

"I'll do my best to comply," Jade mumbled, frowning, accepting the envelope. "I've let so many people down. What will my fans think when this story breaks?"

"Don't despair. Fans never give up on their stars, so you shouldn't give up on yourself, either."

"Thank you for your kindness. I didn't expect it."

Sighing, Patty walked around the reception desk, her arms soon hugging Jade in a compassionate regard. "Aw darling," she whispered in her ear, "I will pray for you."

The tears began again, but Jade quickly wiped at the seepage, stepping away from the embrace.

"Thank you. I don't deserve your kindness."

"Don't be silly," Patty said, shaking her head. "I'm confident the Agency will see you again. A star as bright as you won't soon fade away."

Anxious to leave, Jade reached for the door handle. "I hope you're right."

Jade pulled the heavy mahogany door open, but paused when she glimpsed a well-dressed young woman sitting in the waiting area. A slim brunette, she wore the latest in Kate Spade fashion. She stared at her cellular device, scrolling up and down with pretty painted fingernails. Maybe the next star waited in the wings of the reception area.

Jade sucked in a quivering breath, remembering her younger

self and her first appointment with her former agent, Dixon Reed. The first real rise in her career, that meeting seemed like it had happened a long time ago…

Jade retreated from the Agency's office for what could be the last time. Having no sense of where she was walking, she ambled along the hallway toward the elevators. When the doors slid wide, she stepped inside the space, absent-mindedly pressed the button and descended to the main floor of the building. She made her escape through the front exit and retreated into a shower of depressive rain.

She hoped she'd be able to keep her promise and return to the Agency. She'd die trying.

CHAPTER 2

*D*ays later, Jade stood on her seventeenth floor balcony, studying the pavement below. The lingering gray clouds further distressed an already dour mood. She wanted to end her miserable excuse of a life. She was a failure, a weak-minded soul lost in her own drama, having forfeited everything that mattered a week ago. Everything!

She leaned against the railing and sucked in a breath, wishing a cigarette was wedged between her fingers. Her right hand gripped cold black metal; her bare foot touched the lower edge. *Where did her poisonous thoughts come from?* She considered climbing over the railing to teeter on the concrete lip, further imagining the ensuing drama playing out in her mind, seventeen floors below.

I could end my suffering…

But how would it feel, falling? Would there be pain when she met the ground? Would she suffer in the end or would her suicide be over quickly? She leaned over the edge and peered downward. Her stomach roiled.

So far to fall, she reflected, contemplating the ground below.

That's when she noticed the damnable lens of a photographer.

She backed away, clinging to life. *What was she attempting? Death wasn't the answer to her problems.* Plus, she wouldn't highlight the front page of the local newspaper with blood splatter and smudged makeup. Irritated, she waved instead, then turned away from further bad decisions and walked through her balcony doorway, returning to her lounge chair inside the penthouse suite.

Reclining, she tapped her fingers against the slim armrest. What would she do now? Look for another place to live? Clean her apartment? *Argh*, she groaned, not a chance in hell. But her maid wasn't likely to return without being paid for her services. Household duties were up to her now, but she hated dragging a vacuum across the carpet and although she liked the smell of Mr. Muscle, she'd rather entertain a crowd with artisanal cheese and wine. *Wine…*

Remembering Dixon, she choked on the thought. *My income, where will it come from?* She knew she owed the Agency money for failed concerts and even her rehabilitation stay. She supposed she could return to the bar circuit. An owner or two might welcome a country star's singing.

A bad idea. Such places only enabled further addiction. But surely a fan remembered their favorite artist and still believed in Jade Carter?

A fan, Jade reflected, remembering her conversation with Dixon. Did she still have fans? Maybe her choices had cost her them, too.

She sighed, then glanced at her kitchen counter where she'd abandoned the manila envelope days ago.

"Aw thank you, Patty," she verbalized aloud, then rose from

the lounge chair, walked to the counter and took hold of the bundle. She opened the package and let various sizes of white envelopes fall to the granite top. Her forehead furrowed with concern as she tossed aside the obvious bills, choosing to open a letter with an unruly script first.

Jade Carter, I love you, you da bomb and I want to marry you…

"Oh yes," Jade snickered, shaking her head, "you and every other lonesome hero." She threw the letter in the recycling bin and reached for the next envelope.

Dearest Jade, my mother recently passed away after suffering from lung cancer. I'm short on cash; can you help?

"Wish I could, dear soul. But I'm short on cash myself." She sent this missive sailing into the bin, too.

"Third one's the charm," she said hopefully, gazing at the envelope. "Fancy," she whispered, contemplating the address, "and expensive, too. What's inside this pretty paper?"

Jade sliced the envelope open with an ivory handled letter opener and unfolded a pretty piece of vellum. She read:

Dear Jade Carter,

I'm a fan of yours! I've admired your singing for years and I've attended many of your concerts. I own all your albums, and there isn't anything I wouldn't do to hear you sing again. This is probably a shot in the dark, given that you're such a big star, but I'm getting married in December and I was wondering…

Well, I thought, what would be better than having Jade Carter sing at my wedding? Gosh, and it would be so cool if you wrote a song for me, too. A gift I'd cherish for a lifetime. But, you probably wouldn't consider such a thing? Or would you?

Roberta, the front desk clerk at The Thurston Hotel told me: What the heck, honey, write Jade. She might say yes? So here I am, writing and pleading, waiting with excitement and anticipation for your reply, hoping—

And you'll be compensated. After all, my father is the mayor of Harmony!

Should you wish to pursue this possibility, contact Wendy Thurston, the events manager at The Thurston Hotel. She is handling the arrangements for the wedding. Simply respond to this letter at the aforementioned Thurston Hotel address, and she will take care of the arrangements and your compensation.

Signed affectionately,

"Riley Hamilton?" Jade mused, scrutinizing the return address. "Thurston Hotel—Harmony, Alberta? How very interesting," she reflected, returning to the patio window while tapping the letter against her leg.

"Who would name a town Harmony?"

"Hmm," she pondered, sighing. "I could use a note or two of harmony in my life, and a new place to live, too. Maybe this is a positive sign? Either that or someone is playing a cruel joke on me."

She frowned, considering the request. Yes, she could sing, but write a song? Jade Carter hadn't written a song lyric in years. Not since—

She shook her head, forcing sad memories away. But she needed the money.

Chewing her lip, Jade gazed at the letter. It occurred to her that all she had to do was send a reply to Wendy Thurston.

"I'll do it," she whispered aloud. "What other choice do I have?"

CHAPTER 3

THE SECOND DAY OF MAY

*J*ade listened to the music resounding from the speakers of her G-Rover, fresh with hope and song: *"Any man of mine, better walk the line—"*

Jade sang along, wailing the tune as she drove the last leg of her journey along the Trans-Canada Highway, headed east to the town of Harmony. She loved the tonality of her voice mixing with Shania Twain's song as the artist's music blasted from the radio. This song was one of her favorites, so she sang the lyrics with gusto while focusing on the road ahead.

Not being one to rise early, she had left Revelstoke late in the morning. By the time she reached Lake Louise, the hour was nearing 2:00 p.m. Stopping at the Samson Mall shops, she purchased a coffee and a bagel from Mountain Bakery and Deli, found a bench with a good view of white-capped mountains, and then sat reflecting on her life and the weather. The day was unseasonably warm for this time of year and she was grateful for the sunshine that buoyed her fair skin and her spirits, as though spring seemed to have sprung, winter could still deliver bitterly cold winds fresh with snow.

Jade shivered thinking about it; grateful she lived in Vancouver. Finishing her bagel, she returned to the Rover, climbed inside the cab and returned to the highway. But she didn't feel like singing anymore. She turned the radio off, preferring the solitude of the mountains and tall spruce that lined the roadway. She smiled while passing a herd of elk, glimpsing a sure sign of spring in the tiny calf trailing behind its mother.

She reached Harmony town limits at 3:30 p.m. and soon thereafter, The Thurston Hotel. Tired, she was grateful when she ushered the stick into park.

Accustomed to being taken care of, she parked her vehicle at the front entrance. She didn't even bat an eye when the valet opened her door.

"Welcome to The Thurston Hotel," a young man said, greeting her joyfully. "Will you be using our valet service or self-parking?"

"Valet," she remarked, placing her keys in his hand and disregarding his arched eyebrows as he scrutinized her appearance. Had he guessed who she was?

"May I assist you with your luggage?"

"Yes, please," Jade replied, not meeting his eyes. "My suitcases are inside the hatch."

She stepped from the car, stretching the kinks from her aching back while taking in the hotel front. With a backdrop of Rocky Mountains rising behind the peaked structure, the hotel had been perfectly situated. It was several stories high, but she barely considered the historic beauty or the sandstone facade.

"The front desk is…"

"Thank you, I'll find it," Jade muttered, walking toward the hotel's front entrance. Soon reaching the mahogany doors, she grabbed the brass handle, pulled the door open and passed through with a purpose in mind, not meeting eyes with anyone as she proceeded to the front desk.

"May I help you?" the desk clerk asked.

"Yes," Jade replied, leaning across the counter. "I'm Jade Carter. I'm here to see Wendy Thurston, but when I called to make arrangements, the person I spoke to said to check in at the front desk."

The woman beamed with joy, her exuberance radiated from her eyes and creased her cheeks. "Jade Carter, as I live and breathe, I never expected this day would arrive. I'm Roberta Smythe. Welcome to Harmony and The Thurston Hotel."

Too much happiness in Harmony, Jade decided, but given some people treated her less than kindly these days, she was grateful for the positive greeting.

"I don't mean to be rude," she whispered, ensuring their conversation wasn't overheard by anyone else, "but I need to check in as quickly as possible to protect my privacy. Oh, and please don't shower me with undue attention just because I'm a star. Serve me like you would assist any other guest."

The smile slipped away. "Well, you don't need to be so forward, honey. It's not every day a woman meets a famous country singer. A woman hardly knows how to respond."

"If you listen to news reports or read social media updates, I'm sure you know I'm not that famous anymore. Have you read the papers lately?"

"Those nasty things?" she tittered, touching Jade's hand,

"they're probably all lies written for the amusement of lesser minds."

Jade shook her head, then gazed downward at her booted feet. The desk clerk's statement of support prompted a slim smile to curve her lips upward. "One or two of those stories might be true."

"It's okay, honey," Roberta remarked, squeezing her fingers. "We all suffer our little problems, but we can overcome anything if we set our minds to it. Why, I was just telling my daughters, Reba and Dolly…"

Jade's eyebrows rose at the name disclosure. She studied the woman closer. "You named your daughters Reba and Dolly?"

Roberta chortled a reply, but when she noticed Jade's amusement, her expression changed to one of anger. "Why? Do you have a problem with my choice of names?"

"Of course not." Jade swallowed, appealing for patience, trying to be considerate. "They're your daughters, not mine."

"Ms. Carter, maybe there was some truth to the stories. Hand me your credit card and I'll process your room. After all, I wouldn't want to keep you waiting."

Feeling like she'd made a terrible mistake, Jade reached inside her Dolce & Gabbana dusty-blue purse and retrieved her wallet. Opening it, she reached inside for her VISA card. Nibbling her lip, she passed the black plastic over.

Roberta swiped the card through the machine. Jade watched, counting the seconds, hoping.

"I'm sorry," Roberta apologized, tapping the plastic against the counter. "There seems to be a problem with your card."

"Pass it back to me," Jade said with a sigh, "I'll give you my MasterCard instead."

"I'm sorry; I can't do that. I'm getting a message to call the bank for authorization. If you wait here, I'll be right back."

She disappeared inside a room near the front desk. "Oh God," Jade moaned, nibbling at her lip. This couldn't be good. Not good at all. The Agency must have cancelled her credit.

Roberta returned with a pair of scissors gripped in her hand. "Gosh, I'm really sorry I have to do this. Especially since I do fancy your musical talent, despite the fact you were rude to me."

"I apologize if I offended you, Ms. Smythe. I'm sure Reba McEntire and Dolly Parton would be honored that you named your daughters after them. Please… give me my card back."

"The bank holding your credit card has asked me to cut it up. I have no other choice but to comply."

"No…" Jade moaned, shaking her head. The anxiety strangled her voice. "I beg of you, please don't."

But Jade watched in horror as the clerk grasped the scissors and cut straight across the plastic. Snap! Two black halves dropped to the counter.

"How could you do that?" Jade bellowed, slamming her hand on the counter. "What will I do now?"

"We could try the MasterCard," Roberta suggested, but Jade recognized the woman's doubt. She didn't say anything as she passed the second card to the clerk; however, she was horrified when that card was declined, too. Embarrassment caused her cheeks to flame a bright hue of pink and her eyes filled with tears while studying the front desk clerk's startled expression.

"I don't know what to say," Jade muttered, her voice quivering. "This has never happened to me before."

"Oh dear," Roberta responded, grasping a tissue and passing it over. "Please don't cry. The Thurston Hotel prides itself with providing excellent customer service and we don't want our guests succumbing to fits of emotion."

Jade dabbed at her tears with the tissue. "This is a new low."

The valet brought her three suitcases, nearly tripping as he approached. "Roberta, let me know the room number and I'll take these cases right up."

"That's okay, Gill. Just place them beside the desk and I'll ensure they're taken care of."

"But," he offered, not understanding the difficult situation. Jade turned away from the bell boy, not wanting anyone to witness her shame, her humiliation, and defeat. It was all she could do to stop the tears from forming in her eyes.

"Never you mind, Gill Landis. Be gone with you. Go walk Killer or something."

"What will I do now? I'm supposed to meet Wendy Thurston to arrange a meeting with Riley Hamilton?"

"Don't worry, honey. I'll call Ben, the hotel manager. He'll know how to handle this situation."

MOMENTS LATER, Jade listened to a serious conversation taking place between the hotel manager Ben Thurston and Roberta Smythe, growing more and more alarmed.

"What do you mean, Wendy doesn't know that Jade Carter is here to see her?"

"Well, she doesn't know, and that's all!"

"What have you done, Roberta? It's time you confessed what's going on here."

Roberta lowered her hands in frustration. "Riley Hamilton and Lilith were in the hotel recently, having a heated discussion about the upcoming wedding. I overheard Riley sharing with her mom that she wanted to enquire if Jade Carter could sing at her wedding. But Lilith, *impossible as always*, wouldn't even consider the idea."

"All right, so this explains why Jade Carter is here, to meet with Riley?"

"Yes and no."

Jade scrutinized both of the hotel employees. "I'm not sure what is happening here."

"We're getting to the bottom of it, Miss Carter. Please bear with us."

"Well, I thought Lilith was being unfair to her daughter, so I went ahead and…"

"What did you do?" Ben asked.

"I did what Riley's mom should have done. I wrote a letter to Miss Carter requesting that she sing at the Hamilton wedding." She brightened, gesturing toward her. "And to my delight, Jade Carter responded. She's standing in our lobby!"

Despite the fact that Ms. Roberta Smythe seemed excited that a country star had arrived at the hotel, Jade shook her head, feeling more and more distraught as the seconds passed. No hope to be found in the town of Harmony after all. She should never have opened that manila envelope.

"If I understand correctly," Jade grumbled, sliding her hand through bright red strands, "Riley Hamilton never wrote me a letter, which I presume means that Wendy Thurston won't be meeting with me either."

"Do you have the letter with you?" Ben asked, his expression serious, but calm.

Jade pulled the envelope from her purse, opened the ivory vellum, then passed the stationery to the manager. He took it and glanced at the handwriting, grimacing. "Roberta, this is Thurston letterhead?"

"But of course it is. Did you think a star like Jade Carter would respond to cheap hand-written envelopes from the drugstore?"

"Roberta, your actions go against hotel policy. You've even gone so far as to use your personal phone number as a point of contact."

"Yes, Ben," she asserted, appealing to him with open palms. "But don't you see, my actions were for the greater good. I should receive the hotel employee of the month award for this achievement."

"I apologize, Miss Carter. Our hotel has inconvenienced you."

"What should I do now?" Jade beckoned, lowering her voice for fear of embarrassment. "Your clerk has cut one of my credit cards and the other has been declined. I have very little money with me. Mr. Thurston, I am ashamed to admit that I'm in dire straits. I can't afford the gas to take me home, nor can I afford the cost of one of your rooms. It pains me to admit this, but singing for Miss Hamilton, well, I really needed the income that a potential gig could gain. Your clerk has put me in a difficult situation."

Roberta beamed, gesturing wildly with her hands. "But this situation can remedy itself to everyone's advantage, as now Jade can meet Riley. We need to let the bride know that Jade is here. She'll be so excited, Ben. And I know Lilith will change her opinions, too, when she hears Jade sing."

Ben sighed, crumpling the letter in his hand. He gazed at her, wearing a serious expression. "I find myself in an awkward situation. Your circumstances are none of my concern, but I won't throw a woman into the cold, country music star or otherwise. It appears my front desk clerk, who loves country music by the way, has lured you to the hotel under false pretenses, which is unfair to you, Miss Carter. It's only right that we compensate you for your trouble."

Jade waited expectantly, hoping. "Thank you, Mr. Thurston."

"But?" he cautioned. "You'll have to earn your stay."

Jade nibbled at her lip. "What are you suggesting?"

"I'll accommodate your stay, provided you sing for my guests."

"I can do that," she agreed, nodding her head.

"That's not the only requirement."

"What more could there be?"

"We're short on help right now. I will take care of your accommodation and meals until this situation is resolved, but I will require you to sing, clean, wait on guests in the dining room, and do whatever is required to earn your stay."

Tears seeped from her eyes. "I don't know what to say."

"Please, don't cry," he said, gazing at her meaningfully. "I will speak with our events manager, Wendy Thurston, on your behalf. No promises, but if Riley Hamilton is a fan of yours, she'll want to meet you."

"Yes," Jade replied, swallowing.

"And please, conduct yourself with tact and a sense of decorum while you're a guest at our hotel; we're not immune from gossip. I know the pack of trouble that follows you. I won't put up with drug dealers on my property."

"I won't be any trouble," Jade replied, shocked at his statement. "I'm trying to clean up my life."

"That's good because I don't like trouble. Trouble is bad for business."

"Gill?" Ben called. "Please take our guest's suitcases to the staff quarters."

"Surely, you would give me a room?"

"I'm sorry for your circumstances, but our rooms must be used for paying guests. Now if you'll excuse me, I have other business to attend to."

"When do you want me to sing?"

The first hint of a smile creased his cheeks and brightened his expression. "I think tonight in the lounge. And if Mrs. A. enjoys the performance, I might even offer you a regular room."

CHAPTER 4

Jade sat on a chair in the Thomas Lounge, trying to reconcile what had happened to her earlier. Alone, she appreciated the quiet. No one interrupted her thoughts. Holding her guitar, she struck the E chord and contemplated the strident tone. She tinkered away, plucking at the strings, tightening and loosening the tuners until each chord sounded just right.

"Can I offer you a drink?"

She gazed upward, momentarily awed by amber eyes, defined cheeks and a full mouth that demanded to be kissed. Sighing, she relaxed her guitar to her lap.

"Will it cost me?"

"Everything has its price, ma'am." He smirked, raising his brows. "But this one is on the house."

"Well then, how about a Perrier with a shot of lime juice."

"A real lady's drink," he chuckled, crossing his arms, staring at her. "A girl like you with brilliant red hair, I'd have guessed you'd prefer a stronger drink."

"A woman like me," she offered, striking a G chord, "gets into trouble when she consumes stronger refreshments."

"Jason Knight," he countered, offering her his hand.

She grasped his fingers, unable to break contact with his amber eyes or shake the sensations that fluttered in her belly. She didn't want to release his fingers. He was certainly a nice distraction from her troubles.

"Jade Carter," she finally mumbled, "country music singer."

"Jade—" he chuckled, shaking his head, grinning. "Although it's a pleasure to meet you, this bartender can't make you a drink if you don't release your hold on my hand."

Thirsty, she licked her lips, refusing to break away from his amused expression, releasing his hand soon after. "Sorry," she said with a laugh, smiling, gazing downward. "It's been a long time."

"Ma'am, are you coming on to me?"

"Mr. Knight, our first introduction is not going well at all. I confess, you're a damn fine specimen of a man, but I'm embarrassing myself."

A smile brightened his expression, making him even more attractive. Jade sucked in a breath.

"It depends on how you look at the situation. From my viewpoint, first impressions seem promising. But, perhaps I should make your drink. I have a job to do, after all."

"I need to earn my keep, too, singing tonight. I'd best continue practicing or my vocal tone will be off."

"Practice away then," he replied, returning to the bar. She couldn't help but watch him go. A nice ass to boot! "What will you be singing for me?"

Jade remembered her promise to her coach about behaviors that could trigger a return to using. She didn't see the harm in flirting with the bartender, but she thought it best to avoid him. She couldn't afford to return to her addiction. Still, he was a prize. A sweet jukebox she'd like to drop a quarter inside and play.

"This song is an oldie of mine, but it's still one of my favorites, I think. The song's called: *Let me down easy.*" She began the riff.

> Let me down easy,
> Let me down slow,
> Don't take me to places,
> I don't wanna go.
> Let me down easy,
> Or, don't let me down at all,
> Don't kiss my lips, love,
> If you're not gonna call.

"Wow!" Jason called to her while she continued strumming the chords. "That's one powerful set of lungs, sung with some real passion."

Jade lowered her head, smiling. Then gazed upward as the bartender came forward again, bringing her drink. "Thank you. It felt good to let my frustrations out."

"I bet. Ben tells me you've had some difficulties lately."

"He told you?" Jade sighed, reflecting on the day and her past. "You could say I've been in the news."

"I don't pay much attention to what's in the papers; in fact, I don't read them anymore. Prefer to spend my time focused on more leisurely pursuits."

Jade smiled, stopped her strumming and reached forward to accept the beverage. Instant heat fired her emotions as their fingers touched. Watching him, she brought the glass to her lips and took a sip, enjoying the bubbly flavor, a simple and satisfying mix.

"Thank you," she offered, then placed the glass on a side table. "Delicious and refreshing."

He nodded his head, and she began singing again, staring purposefully at his amber eyes.

> Love me easy,
> Love me slow,
> Kiss my full lips, love,
> Don't let me go.
> I see that you want her,
> I see your need,
> My heart is aching,
> Don't make me bleed—

"Who hurt you?" he asked, staring at her like he was reaching inside her soul.

Uncomfortable with the question, Jade glanced downward, then placed her guitar on the stand. "It's just a song, Jason. A sentimental melody I awoke to after a long night of drinking."

"I've heard there's a grain of truth to every singer's song, but maybe your story's true," he murmured, kneeling in front of her. "But the tone of your voice and the way you sang, the way you glanced away when I looked at you, tells me there might be a deeper meaning hidden inside your lyrics; a discomfort, too. But we've just met. Share your truth when you're ready to."

Jade reflected that she'd like to share much more than a song with this man, but she needed to escape the rising tension. Her heart was pounding.

"My vocal cords are warmed up. I'm ready to sing for the Thurston clientele, but I'm going to find something to eat and then take in the peace and tranquility of the mountains before my set."

"If you want a light meal, The Alberta Rose Coffee Shop has meals to go. Maybe you'd like to visit the garden on the South side of the building," he offered, rising, stepping away. "The tulips have just begun to bloom."

"Sounds perfect. Thank you for your kindness."

"You're welcome. I'll see you later. Now that I've heard you sing, I'm looking forward to the rest of your set."

It had been so long since anyone had shown her kindness or compassion, that Jade simply studied his serene expression with a growing sense of surprise and wonder. She sighed, smiled slightly, and nodded her head in gratitude, then went in search of the coffee shop he'd mentioned; though she didn't feel like eating. This day had been one big note of uncertainty and this man had been the only light to add joy to her downhearted spirit.

Who are you, Jason Knight?

CHAPTER 5

*H*oly hell, Jason reminded himself as he stocked the bar for the evening customers—the singer was a fox! Right from the moment he first saw her, she'd commanded his attention with her beauty, her painted face, and a voice that could lull a baby to sleep. But Ben Thurston was probably correct in his estimation that Jade Carter was trouble, trouble that a man like himself could hardly afford to consider. But a light shining in her hazel eyes, glistening pink on full lips, had him wanting to know more about the singer.

Back away, Jason, he told himself as the customers began entering the lounge. But ignoring this woman was the last action Jason had in mind. If anything, he wanted to press closer and get to know her better.

Mrs. A. sidled up to the bar and sat on an upholstered barstool. "Good evening, Jason."

"Good evening to you, Mrs. A." Jason said, wiping the bar top clean. "What can I get you?"

"My usual. Vodka on the rocks with a lemon wedge," she

said, reflecting on the people around her. "Any luck with the private investigator?"

For a fleeting moment, Jason wondered how he had let Mrs. A. convince him to go along with her farfetched plan. She wanted to find Mrs. Jamieson's lost daughter—lost for over thirty years. He leaned closer to Mrs. A., lowering his voice. "I gave him the picture of Emily—I mean, Mrs. Jamieson. The one taken when she was fifty years old."

"Her fiftieth birthday picture." Mrs. A. smiled. "That's a lovely photo."

"Yes, it is. And that's how old the daughter would be now, right?"

"Right," Mrs. A. answered. "And? What did the PI say?"

"The PI could use a name."

"Her name is Mary Jamieson. You know that."

Jason sighed. "If she married, she might have changed her name."

"Oh yes, I do believe you're right." Mrs. A. frowned, swirling her drink, watching the ice cubes spin around in her glass. "But how could we possibly figure out who she married?"

Jason wondered if he should keep assisting Mrs. Arbuckle with the search. It was tedious. Though he admired and respected this woman and would do anything to keep her happy. "There's a good chance there was a boyfriend involved when the young Mary Jamieson ran way."

"Of course! That makes sense. So I need to learn the boyfriend's name."

"Yes, you do."

"I can do that."

"You still haven't told Emily—Mrs. Jamieson—what you're up to?"

"No, I haven't told her anything. If we're unable to find her daughter, I don't want her to be disappointed."

"Of course," Jason offered, seeing they were soon to be interrupted. "We'll talk about this again, soon."

Roberta approached the bar in a hurry and took a seat. "Have you heard who's singing tonight?" she exclaimed, leaning against the bar top. "None other than country music sensation, Jade Carter."

"I've met her. I've heard her sing, too," Jason replied, placing Mrs. A's drink in front of her. "What can I get you, Roberta?"

"A mint julep, but go light on the bourbon."

Jason shook his head as he muddled the mint. He knew Jade had traveled to Harmony and The Thurston Hotel because of the meddling of this woman. Ben had told him as much. He imagined she meant well, as he added an extra splash of bourbon, touching up the drink with a spritz of club soda for fizz.

"Gosh," Roberta said, grinning, "I'm her biggest fan. I can't wait to hear her sing."

"Is that so," Mrs. A. replied, sipping her drink, "I've never heard of her."

"Never heard of her?" Roberta shrieked, clasping the senior's arm. "Mrs. A., you need to get around more."

"Roberta!" Mrs. A. countered, shrugging off the embrace. "I've seen enough in my life. Right now, I'd rather hear Jade so-and-so sing than listen to you disturbing my nightly medicinal."

Jason chuckled under his breath. "There are two free tables near the stage, Roberta. I think one of them has your name on it."

"Jason, are you trying to get rid of me?"

"Just trying to keep the customers satisfied, ma'am. Come

with me," he suggested with a wink, offering her his arm. "I'll escort you to a table. I'll bring your drink over, too."

Not one to be shy, Roberta embraced his arm. "Too bad you're working tonight, honey. You could take the chair beside me."

"That's kind of you to invite me." Jason coughed into his hand, trying not to laugh. "But if I don't earn my keep, Ben will fire me."

"I don't think so," Mrs. A. hastened to say, raising her glass to him. "Good help is hard to find. Good friends, even harder."

After Roberta took her seat, Riley Hamilton walked into the lounge with her parents, Mr. and Mrs. Hamilton. They sat at the table nearest to the stage, and Jason approached them there.

"Fancy seeing the Hamiltons' at the Thurston on a Monday night."

Riley smiled at him, her eyes twinkling with delight. "Roberta told me that Jade Carter was singing tonight. I can't believe it."

"It was a surprise to me too," Jason mentioned, scratching his head. "She was practicing earlier, warming up for the show tonight. From what I heard, you won't be disappointed."

Lilith rolled her eyes. "I can't believe Riley dragged me here."

"Stop, Mom. You might enjoy the music."

"How about I get you a drink?" Jason offered. "The music will speak for itself."

"Thank you," Riley said. "I'll have a glass of CedarCreek Riesling."

"My husband and I will share a bottle of the CedarCreek Merlot," Lilith Hamilton stated.

Jason winced at the thought. The red wine held a

characteristic of fruitcake, but hey, maybe the Hamiltons' enjoyed a good fruitcake.

"Wait a minute," Riley blurted, "I've changed my mind. I'll have the Hillside Rose. I want to show my mother that I'm open to change, but that I still understand the importance of tradition."

"The choice of wine can say a lot about the connoisseur," Jason hinted, understanding that unlike the red and white choices of fermented grapes, life was infinitely more complicated. "I myself prefer a traditional beer."

"Me, too." Edward Hamilton chuckled. "But Lilith here, likes to take the lead."

"Edward—" Lilith complained.

Jason knew he shouldn't intrude; he gritted his teeth. "I can get you one?"

"No, that's okay. It's best to stay with the tried and true. A complex vintage with notes as sweet and smooth as my dear wife."

Lilith's head lowered, her cheeks flamed pink and a broad grin brightened her eyes.

"As you wish," Jason continued. "I'll get your wine right away."

He attempted to return to the bar, but halfway between his intended destination and the stage, Jason paused—Jade Carter had entered the room.

He watched her as she walked through the lounge, scrutinizing her slim figure as she sauntered between the seated guests and the tables. He knew she had been a vision before, but now with artful makeup highlighting hazel eyes, bright red hair curling past her shoulders, and wearing a beaded red dress that sparkled within the dimly lit room—well, now she was a beauty.

His observation gave way to creamy white shoulders and a tempting décolletage…

Don't stare, he remembered his manners, swallowing as she glanced his way. Noticing her full red lips, he licked his own. *Walk to the bar, Jason, walk to the bar. Stop obsessing in regard to this beautiful woman!*

Don't watch her pick up the guitar.

Don't stare at her delicate fingers strumming the guitar strings, giving rise to song.

An ache stirring in his gut became stronger when she began to sing:

Let me down easy—

Though Jason didn't know what emotion compelled his hidden desires, one simple goal motivated his attention; he wanted more than a sad song from Jade Carter.

CHAPTER 6

Jade retrieved her guitar from its stand, then sat on a stool situated in the middle of the stage, the black base more a platform than a performance space. She appraised the small gathering of people, suffering a moment of awkward silence; the interval between the star attraction and their song, and the audience who waited for the performance to begin. She glanced at the desk clerk. Roberta smiled at her but the modest grin didn't offer comfort, if it was meant to. Sitting near her at a separate table, a woman dressed in richer clothing placed her fingertips on her lips, expressing an excited sentiment in the action. Jade had witnessed such enthusiasm before. Maybe this woman was the bride who she had come to meet?

A small group wearing matching blazers, three women and one man, walked into the lounge next. Jade recognized the manager who had assisted her this afternoon. She took a deep breath, not understanding why she felt so stressed. She tried to shake the overwhelming nervousness, rolling her shoulders backward to release the strain, then she strummed the first chords, ensuring the guitar was in tune before she sang.

Seeing Jason Knight across the lounge, she pondered the man standing behind the mahogany bar top, holding a glass in his hand and swirling the amber liquid inside round and round. She reflected on their earlier introduction, remembering the song she'd sung. She hadn't planned on singing *Let me down easy,* and she didn't know why she was about to share it with the audience now.

The song brought back memories of a time in her life when her troubles had been greatest, a time before cigarettes, drugs and booze. She was trying to change her future, trying to reshape her life, but to do that she had to revisit the past. She took a deep breath and began to sing.

Let me down easy—

Suddenly, no audience member disrupted her silence; she was one with the music, her voice, a guitar and her song.

Let me down slow.

Why did you do it, Taylor? She considered, strumming. Why did you let me go?

Don't take me to places, I don't wanna go.

She still missed her former flame; the unresolved feelings twisted inside her gut like a knife wedged within her heart. The pain deepened as she sang, robbing her voice and stealing air from her lungs, causing panic.

Let me down easy, *she ground out.*

Or, don't let me down at all,
Don't kiss my lips, love,
If you're not gonna call.

Taylor, I need to forget what you did to me. Jade paused, sighed, and then quit singing. She reached for the microphone after a shuddering breath and began to talk.

"I wrote *Let me down easy* early in my career. It's a sad ballad of lost love, and I'm not sure why I sang it tonight."

The well-mannered audience simply stared at her, not one person saying as much as a tiny whisper. They waited patiently for her to speak.

"Perhaps, I'll continue with some happier tunes from what I hope won't be my last album."

Jade sang: *You gotta hold on to me, Riddled with Fear* and *Bad Boys of Music City.* She hated all three songs. Written for her by three separate artists, they were smitten with substandard lyrics. She could tell that the audience didn't like them. *Too quiet,* they were too quiet by far. No one clapped. No one sang along. People gazed at the ceiling or peered at their shoes, waiting patiently for the music to die away. A few people got up and left. Jade was ready to cry.

The audience didn't appreciate her gift. She sighed as she finished: *One stupid fool.*

A senior woman sitting at the bar, rose from a barstool and approached the minor stage. Carrying a drink, she took a seat beside Roberta.

"Jade Carter?" she called out during the pause. "Do you think you could sing a song by Patsy Cline? Maybe share some *Sweet Dreams* with us before I retire for the night?"

Jade rested her guitar on her lap. "I know the song, but it's not part of my list."

"Can you sing it?"

"I'll try," Jade replied, repositioning the guitar. She fiddled with the chords, considering where to start. Key of A, she thought, and began.

"Sweet—" she drawled out, stretching the note for as long as she could. "Dreams of you—"

"Every night," she whimpered. "I go through."

Why can't I forget the past and begin my life anew?

Where did the emotion come from? She felt the tears pooling in her eyes, the sorrow etching her heart, and when she reached the second verse—Jade remembered: Taylor hadn't loved her at all and she should have known better than to fall for him.

By the third verse the tears were sliding down her cheeks and her voice began to wobble. So upset, she cursed herself for destroying Patsy's song. She should never have sung *Let me down easy,* as memories had emerged with that silly old song, ruining everything. And just like her recent past, she was letting her personal life intrude on a beautiful song.

"Why?" she sang, sobbing, "Why can't I forget the past and love someone new?"

When she finished, she closed her eyes, gasping for breath, sucking air inside her lungs. She was surprised to hear the sound of applause. She contemplated the audience with tears welling in her eyes, feeling undeserving of the recognition. She noticed that the older woman in the front row was smiling, wearing an earnest expression and applauding the performance, too. Roberta was standing on her feet, clapping crazily.

Jason openly stared at her. The man was obviously in shock, his expression too much for her to cope with.

"Thank you," she whispered into the microphone, her voice uneven, "that's all for tonight."

And then, she placed her guitar on the stand and retreated from the stage, walking at first and then rushing across the floor, hurrying through the lobby, nearly running when she reached the stairs to the basement. Returning to the staff quarters where the manager had been kind enough to let her stay. It was a new low living in a basement. Oh dear, how far she had fallen.

JASON PLACED his glass on the bar top, prepared to drop everything and rush to the singer. Heartbreak and other issues related to the heart were subjects he understood well, having suffered his own health scare. Her sorrow reached inside his chest and squeezed at his beating heart. He'd just met Jade Carter, but he wanted to pursue the country star and return the smile to her pretty face.

Ben grasped his arm. "Let her go, Jason. She's not your girlfriend, not even a friend. A stranger to us all, really."

"But Ben, she's hurting. And she's alone."

"She's safe. Whatever she's facing inside, she needs to work through the emotions."

"Oh, and is that what you did with Melanie? You worked through the emotions?"

"That and more," Melanie responded, reaching for Ben's hand. "But in this instance, I'm on Ben's side. You don't know Jade Carter. Let her go. Let her be."

"You're really *riddled with fear*, Jason."

"That's not funny, Ben," Jason replied, shaking his head. "Can someone check on her, make sure she's okay?"

Riley Hamilton interrupted. "I don't mean to intrude on your conversation, but maybe I can help. Roberta told me about Jade's troubles and the situation that brought her to Harmony. I want to help her. After all, she's my favorite country music star."

"That's kind of you," Jason said.

"Please tell her I'd like to meet with her to discuss singing at my wedding. Wendy, can you make the arrangements?"

"Yes, Riley," Wendy agreed, standing near Melanie and Ben. "It would be my pleasure."

"I need to check my schedule, but I'd like to meet with Jade as soon as possible," Riley remarked, clearly thinking about the prospect. "Maybe later this week?"

"That works for me," Wendy answered. "I'll make the arrangements as soon as I know your schedule."

"Jason?" Riley began. "Maybe you should share the good news with Jade? I can see you want to."

"I should, shouldn't I?"

Ben chuckled. "Don't look at me. You're the one entertaining a whole pack of trouble."

"Ben, can you watch the bar?"

"If you're set on getting hurt."

"I'm not about to make a marriage proposal, but didn't you see her tears? I only want to ensure she's comforted."

"Of course you do," Ben bantered, an amused look lighting his eyes. "Well, you've been my bridge during difficult times, so I suppose I have no choice but to support you. But don't drown the woman with your caring attitude. *Let her down easy,* Jason."

"You had to say that, didn't you." Jason shook his head and walked past his best friend. But Ben had a point. What was he getting himself into? Right now, he only wanted to find the singer. He had to help her, if he could.

Jason was surprised to find Jade lounging on a cot in the staff room only wearing her undergarments. She had removed her sparkly attire and sat on the bed dressed in a red sequined bra with matching panties. She twisted his way when he approached.

"I'm sorry," he mumbled, turning away from her exposed beauty.

"It's no matter," she said with a sigh, drawing her fingers across pink cheeks fresh with tears. Mascara had smudged the hollows beneath her eyes and gray liquid slid down her face. "You're not seeing anything others have not seen before."

"I'm a gentleman. I don't take advantage of women."

"I won't bite, turn around."

He did as she asked, soon staring at her breasts rising above the bra. Like a deer caught in the headlights of a car, a man bewitched by a sexy siren couldn't refrain from staring at the light.

She lifted her lips into a semblance of a smile. "Oh dear, I see what you're thinking: that I'm some kind of immodest woman. It's nothing like that. After an entertainer finishes a show, you're so warm from the lights that the first action you take is to remove the costuming. There are often so many people crowded inside the dressing room that a girl doesn't have privacy. I've developed a thick skin when changing from my costumes, so sitting in front of you in my underwear is permissible from an entertainment standard. I'm comfortable, you should be too."

Jason placed his back to her. "Ma'am, this man is a gentleman and I'm not used to seeing too many women half-naked like this." He swallowed, sucking in a breath. "I confess, you're gorgeous, but maybe you should put some clothes on."

"If you say so," she replied. He heard the springs of the bed creak as she rose. "Give me a minute, Jason. I'll put my robe on."

He waited patiently, his temperature rising. He didn't really want her to get dressed. "Are you decent?"

"Yes," she whispered.

He turned in time to see her sit back down on the bed, soon tying a length of fabric around a red silk robe, the silk hugging the sweet curves of her figure. But he could still glimpse a tiny strip of red and the creamy valley that lay between her breasts. He licked his lips.

"I wanted to make sure you were okay."

She appeared wounded and stared at him compellingly.

"Another horrible performance," she breathed, gazing at her hands on her lap. "My audience has come to expect disappointment from me."

Jason walked to the opposite cot and sat down; he soon leaned toward her. "You were not terrible."

"You're a kind man, but I know who and what I am. The audience deserved better. What brings you here, you should be tending the bar?"

"I told you, I wanted to make sure you were okay."

"I'm fine," she declared, almost too loudly. But Jason saw by the way her lip quivered that she was anything but fine. He reached to her and placed his hand on her silk-dressed shoulder. Only to offer his support, he told himself, but human need reared inside him with desire and purpose. She saw his weakness, too.

What the hell, Jason. Why are you here?

"I see what you want," she whispered, offering no sign of emotion. "You're a man like any other. To me, you're like a drug; I could easily consume you."

"I didn't come here to go to bed with you."

"Didn't you?"

"Jade, you're one hell of a fox, but I'm not that type of guy. I don't take advantage of women. Nor do I jump into bed with the first beautiful girl who tempts me."

She stretched forward. "There aren't too many men anymore that hold any form of chivalry. What kind of man are you? Are you a knight in shining armor kind of man, Jason Knight? Here to court me, save me from a dangerous foe?"

"Do you see any chain mail, darling?"

"Not a single link," she sighed, face upturned, and too responsive to his proximity. "But I do like what I see."

Her sensuality aroused his desire, but this situation needed to be calmed before it burst into flames. "That decides it then. It's safer to return to why I came here in the first place."

"Because you care about me?"

Jason strived for control while reflecting on Jade's pessimistic attitude. "An important client of the hotel watched you sing tonight. She was impressed with your performance."

"Which part, the place where my voice croaked like a frog, or where I blubbered the last lines of *Sweet Dreams*? Patsy Cline would not have been amused."

Thinking it unwise, Jason sat beside her on the cot. She didn't even flinch, as if she were accustomed to men sitting beside her on a bed. Geez, was she that easy? He questioned this. "You really think the worst, don't you?"

She leaned toward him, and blatantly touched his lips with

her index finger. "Are you going to kiss me, Jason? Or just tease me, sitting this close?"

He leaned in. "Her name is Riley Hamilton."

"The woman who wants me to sing at her wedding?"

"One and the same. She wants to arrange a meeting sometime this week. Do you think you're up to that?"

The first hint of a smile played on her lips. "Do you think you're up to kissing me; helping me forget my past?"

He chuckled, glimpsing the return of light to her eyes, but he left the seat of temptation and backed away. "I think it's best I get back to tending the bar. It's far too hot down here."

She leaned backward. "Another time, Jason Knight?"

She sparkled so pretty he couldn't help himself. "I'm not working Friday night. We could get to know each other better. I could show you the sights, help you discover our little town of Harmony?"

"I'd like that."

"Well then, I'd best let you get some rest."

"Jason," she whispered, pulling the satin robe across her sweet chest, "thank you."

"Don't thank me, not just yet." He glanced away momentarily. "The events manager of the hotel will arrange your meeting with the bride. Wendy will be in contact with you."

"You're too good to be true. I can't wait to see what else the town of Harmony has to offer."

"Good night, Jade. Sleep well."

"Sweet dreams, Jason. See you soon."

He left her then and approached the stairs that would take him to the main floor of the hotel. *A date?* He was committed now and knew he couldn't withdraw from his plans. In a few days, he would get to know Jade Carter on a more personal level.

He hoped he could control his male behavior and act like a gentleman.

Who was he kidding; the woman was a spark-plug, the ignition sequence firing his emotions, and he didn't want to control anything. Friday couldn't come soon enough!

CHAPTER 7

*J*ade awoke to the persistent buzzing of a woman's voice. "Jade, Jade—" Someone chirruped, nudging her arm. "Time to wake up, mate. Time to get your day started."

"Leave me alone!" Jade grumbled, squeezing her eyes shut tight and pulling the comforter over her head. "It's not time to get up."

But the nuisance whipped the covers from her body. "According to Mr. Thurston, you're the new help. The gent sent me to wake you. So rise and shine, my beauty. It's time to greet a new day."

Suddenly cold, and angry too, Jade rolled onto her back and opened her eyes. She scrutinized a young blonde woman with wispy hair wafting around her pretty face. Baby blue eyes shone with pleasure, and to some degree, a touch of mischief, too. The cheeky woman had the audacity to smile.

"And what angel has roused me from the grips of a nightmare?"

"Nightmare? If that's where you were lolling, it's for the best

I saved you from your sleep." She smiled brightly. "Jade Carter, I'm Poppy Ellis. It's a pleasure to meet you."

Jade groaned, crossing her arms against her chest. "Really, it's a pleasure?"

"Has anyone told you that you're a grumpy woman in the morning? Perhaps you should go to bed earlier. Come on, sit up, I've brought you some brekkie."

Still wearing her red silk robe from the night before, Jade rubbed the sleep from her eyes and rose to a sitting position on the tiny cot, swinging her legs over the side. Now that she was more awake, she considered Poppy Ellis.

"Where are you from, Poppy? I hear the accent in your voice. The UK, or are you an Australian?"

She giggled, reaching for a covered plate. "I'm from Sydney, Australia, mate. I'm here in your beautiful Rocky Mountains for a year."

"Snowboarder?"

"In the winter. When summer arrives, I want to try the mountain bike trails, might even ride down the lower hills to face my demons."

"Has the season ended yet?"

"Not yet. Sunshine's still open, but the powder's gone. It's a slush festival up there right now. But I'll bear the ride, regardless of packed powder or slush-snow, until the season ends. But Mr. Thurston didn't send me here to talk about my recreational activities. It's time for you to get dressed and have a coffee, 'cause we have rooms to clean, my beauty."

"Were you born happy, Poppy Ellis? Has anyone told you that such unbridled cheerfulness this early in the morning is frightfully annoying?"

"Ms. Carter," she preached, giggling, "it's long past nine! I start work at eight. Given that we're short-staffed right now, Mr. Thurston let you sleep an entire extra hour. He's a good man, but I'm looking forward to your helping hands."

"Well," Jade complained, "I worked last night."

"Your singing?" Poppy chuckled, raising her eyebrows. "From what I heard, you should have come with me to The Wobbly Dog for an amber. I know how to have a good time."

"I'm sure you do, Poppy. But, I'm staying away from the bar scene."

"It's not a bar; it's a pub. A place to sit back and unwind from the day's troubles, share a glass or two with a friend and talk about the news, the weather, and the joys of life. It's about community, Jade."

"It's a bar in Canada, darling. A place to purchase a joint or pick up a date, if you get my meaning."

"You have a vivid imagination," Poppy said casually, passing a cup of coffee over. "I don't know about the dating options in Harmony as I have not seen too many approachable Canadian boys on the hill, but I'm always open to new friends." She winked suggestively.

Jade sighed, then accepted the only addiction she could consume without regret, taking a sip. "Nice," she mumbled, savoring the smooth, satisfying flavor, grateful her new work associate had added milk. She took a deep breath then caught Poppy's attention. "Look, I appreciate your kindness on my behalf, but I'm not at my best this early in the morning, so we should limit the small talk," Jade stated, climbing from the bed and carrying her coffee, "at least until I'm more awake. I'm nicer when my mind is alert. Let me get dressed."

"Do you want to eat first? I brought you a hearty breakfast. Eggs, sausage and hashed browns."

Jade wrinkled her nose. "It's too early for food and I've never been one to eat unhealthy carbs or fatty meats."

Poppy sighed, clearly exasperated. "I personally believe that eggs are an excellent source of protein. They'll keep you satisfied with the hard work ahead of us."

"If you say so," Jade grumbled, but she gave in, reluctantly accepting the covered plate and cutlery from Poppy, then she sat on the bed and placed her coffee on the end table. She sat comfortably, the plate resting on her lap. When she removed the lid, she was surprised to see a vegetarian omelette, and though she didn't feel hungry, the aroma enticed her. She ate a forkful of the omelette.

"How do you like it?" Poppy asked, taking a seat. "Pam Sheridan made your breakfast. She's an excellent chef."

"It's delicious," Jade said, taking a second bite. "I suppose I'm hungrier than I thought." Jade had soon eaten the entire omelette, one sausage, and a bite of the hash-browns.

"When you've finished your breakfast, I'll teach you some work responsibilities as well as the joyful life of cleaning hotel rooms for a living."

Jade groaned again, chewing. "Sounds delightful."

"I have a uniform for you to wear, too."

"Brilliant!" Jade griped, swallowing. The hashed browns were really good. "You've thought of everything." She placed an almost empty plate on the side table.

Poppy tossed her a pile of emerald cotton. "Let's get going," she said, a huge smile on her face. "Phish posh, time to set off."

Jade dressed quickly, removing her red silk robe and pulling on an emerald-green cotton shirt and pants that reminded her of a hospital uniform. She certainly wasn't about to make a fashion statement wearing this unsightly garb, but she supposed the garments would at least be comfortable. She shook her head. This was going to be a long day!

WHEN THE GUEST rooms were clean, Jade was able to do as she wished with her free time. But her arms ached from pushing the monstrous cleaning cart over-loaded with towels, bed sheets, and sundry items. Most of the articles had been stacked higher than she could reach. Not to mention that her fingers were raw from scrubbing sinks, tubs, and worst of all, toilets. She probably reeked of pine and lemon-scented cleaning fluid.

Too tired to change out of the uniform, she sat in the Margaret Library on an antique sofa, gazing at bric-a-brac and shelves lined with books and the odd magazine. Sipping tea, she reflected on her day.

One element of her labor waxed important: she had to restore her career, as she couldn't see herself living her life as a maid! My goodness, she was weary to the bone and her eyelids kept drooping. In the past few days, she'd acquired an entirely new appreciation for this laborious job. For certain, if she ever regained her career, she was tipping the housekeeping attendants!

I'll only close my eyes for a minute, she thought, but she succumbed to sleep anyway, right there on the sofa.

"Jade…" a masculine voice whispered in her ear.

"Jade?" She felt fingertips slide across her cheek. "It's time to wake up."

"Taylor?" she responded. "Why?"

She felt a weight on the sofa, but she couldn't open her eyes. *Too tired,* she reflected.

"It's not Taylor. Hey, I thought we had a date?"

She opened her eyes, seeing the man she had met her first day at the hotel. Jason gazed back at her wearing a tight black T-shirt and a quizzical expression. Amber eyes, defined cheeks and full kissable lips. She wanted to draw her fingers through his short black hair. Sighing, she gazed at his chest. The man could be a Chippendale dancer.

"Jason?"

"I promised to show you the town, but here I find you asleep. Are you too tired?"

"I'm sorry," she apologized, rubbing her eyes. "Poppy worked me hard. I guess I fell asleep."

"Do you want to cancel?"

She sighed again, her heartbeat fluttering. "No, I don't want to cancel. In fact, it would be good to stretch my legs. What do you have in mind?"

"A walk beside Harmony Creek. I have a picnic basket filled to the brim with a selection of artisan cheese, dessert, some Perrier and limes and a dinner for two."

"You have a picnic basket? You did that for me?"

"I'm a capable man. Why don't you change into something, ah, more comfortable? Then we'll be on our way."

"You don't like my uniform?" Jade giggled, teasing, punching him playfully on the arm.

He shook his head, his comical expression saying no way, please change. "I don't mind the green, if it makes you happy. It's a beautiful day, unseasonably warm for this time of year. The sun sets early and the temperature can drop, making it cold, so bring a sweater."

Jade rose from the sofa, pausing only to study the interest in his eyes. "I won't be long."

"I'll be waiting."

~

JADE CHANGED into a white pair of jeans and a black chiffon blouse. She left the Thurston staff room carrying her baby-blue purse and a bright pink cashmere sweater with a white-checkered pair of Louis Vuitton sneakers on her feet. Then, she climbed the staircase to the main floor of The Thurston Hotel with every leg muscle cramping.

Ouch! She'd never grow accustomed to this type of living.

She found Jason waiting for her in the lobby. He appeared awkward and studied her in a quizzical way while holding a wicker picnic basket and a woolen blanket. She couldn't remember anyone assuming such a kindness for her. She smiled, and a giggle escaped her lips.

"Don't look so surprised," he replied, stepping toward her. "Here, you carry the blanket and I'll carry the basket."

"Certainly," she replied, accepting the blanket from his outstretched hands, and folding the length over her arms. She glanced at his amber eyes as they walked past the seating area next to the lobby, soon passing the Thomas Lounge where she had sung the night before. Eventually, they left the hotel through a side entrance. Soon, they were meandering through the Thurston gardens, walking toward the bridge.

"Who is Taylor?" Jason asked.

Jade nibbled at her lip, glancing away, her thoughts stretching beyond the gravel pathway of fuchsia tulips and purple pansies. She didn't want to answer the question.

"Why do you ask?"

"You whispered his name in your sleep."

Pausing on the pathway, she gazed at his eyes and saw a genuine interest. "An old boyfriend," she sighed, not wanting to talk about her past. "I don't usually confide my personal life with strangers. Attention to privacy is a best kept practice in the business."

"Don't worry, I'm not a member of the paparazzi. I won't divulge any secrets you choose to reveal. And if I had a camera, I'd only point the lens at the trees."

"Are you certain?" she asked, walking again, approaching a wooden bridge that spanned the creek. "You wouldn't take a photo of me? A man such as yourself could earn top dollar if you shared my secrets with the right news outlet."

He stepped onto the wooden bridge. "I'm comfortable in my financial affairs. I don't need to share your private life for the almighty coin. I'll only share what's inside the picnic basket, and that's all. No secrets, scout's honor!"

Jade stopped in the middle of the bridge, her back resting on the railing, her hands clasped to her chest. "Is that so? Your motives are pure? In my situation, I have found that men and women equally want something more than I can provide. Whatever lingers in your basket, I fear the contents will have their cost in time."

"You have a strong spirit, Jade, and an even stronger imagination."

"What do you want from me? Why did you trouble yourself to prepare a picnic dinner in the first place?"

A pure masculine force, he stepped toward her, scrutinizing her face. My goodness, a woman could drown in his eyes etched with gold. She could smell his musk cologne, an aftershave as rich as the luxury shoes on her feet. The drug crying out within her soul and screaming to be fed reared its ugly head. She needed to resist him, but oh, how she wanted to taste his lips. What could it hurt?

"I'm not sure what I want," he confessed, "but, I'll admit that it's unusual for me to go to such lengths to entertain a woman I've only just met. I bought the basket this afternoon."

"So, you admit it." She chuckled, surprised at his temerity. "You do want something from me."

"I'll admit that I want to learn more about you, and I'm prepared to cross the creek to see if my interest can be satisfied."

"Huh," Jade said, turning toward the supports that extended over the bridge. She glanced at his expression, and then began walking to the other side of the creek. "We're in trouble, Jason. I want to see what's inside your basket."

He followed so close beside her that she felt the heat of his body. "I've piqued your interest?"

"Yes," she replied as they passed beneath a white arbor, "I want to satisfy your curiosity, but the wrong response could earn us some trouble."

His laughter drifted with the wind, the sound as sweet as the trill of a tiny thrush. "I've never shied away from trouble."

His fingers stroked her hand and the impact of his touch caused her skin to quiver. "That's good, for I fear you're about to meet some."

JASON TOOK the blanket from Jade's hands and stretched it over freshly mown grass, a distance away from the creek's shoreline. With tall trees and green shrubbery surrounding them, the area seemed private. Soon lying underneath a tall poplar tree, he was not only grateful for the solitude, but also appreciated that no other townsfolk had chosen to picnic here, too. Most people would stray to the gazebo instead. Here, they were quite alone.

"Make yourself comfortable," Jason offered, contemplating Jade. She sat on the blanket, stretching onto her side, dropping her pink sweater on the ground. He noticed the flimsy black blouse. The top portion had a band of sheer fabric; he glimpsed the creamy rise of her breasts beneath the folds. Swallowing, he tried to stem his longing.

She had the audacity to smile as if she'd noticed his interest. A vixen, she lay on the ground, the leaves rustling, flirting with the wind, and he couldn't turn away from her hazel eyes or her bright pink painted lips, which he wanted to taste, to kiss.

"You've become quiet," she said.

He glanced away, better to distract himself from his need by opening the basket. "Just deep in thought, singer."

"Is that so? Your brow is furrowed with stress," Jade offered, her fingers twisting a blade of grass. "Why should one stress in such a place?" She stretched backward, closing her eyes. "It's been a long time since I could relax like this and listen to the songs of birds. Thank you for bringing me here."

He sighed, glanced away, then opened the basket lid. "You're welcome. We should eat."

She opened her eyes, again, her scrutiny causing his heart to flutter. "Are you hungry?"

"Yes, I am. But if I didn't know better, I'd think you were purposefully tempting me. The warmth in your eyes, the way your hand stirs on the blanket, almost as if..."

"I'm twenty-eight years old and I'm not a virgin. If you're hungry for something other than food, I might be willing."

"Jade—" Jason declared, making a face, "I've never met a woman as forward. I'm not sure what to make of you?"

She rose and crawled forward on her knees to sit beside him. Her knees brushed against his; she touched his grizzled cheeks, her fingers gently embracing his face, tempting him. "Everything in its proper time, but for now, let's eat. One should never move too fast. Discretion is the key to valor."

"Is it?" he asked, grasping the lid of the basket. "You're tempting me to think otherwise."

"So my counselor tells me," Jade replied honestly.

"Hmm," Jason said, removing a cutting board from the basket. He plied it with various wedges of cheese, olives, a baguette of bread and a knife. "I've never wanted to neglect the code of honor more in my life."

He looked at her. "Jade, you're a dish I'd like to taste."

Comfortable, she reached for a bite of cheese and placed it inside her mouth. "Taste me then. End your suffering."

He leaned toward her, so close he could smell her floral perfume. A brave woman, she didn't back away. He gave her every opportunity to do so, waited for her to say no while staring at her hazel eyes. She pressed closer, reached out with her tongue and licked his lips.

"You taste far richer than the cheese. What are you waiting for? Stoke your advantage."

He kissed her, welcoming the soft tissues beneath his lips, then thinking better of such temptation, backed away, resting on his haunches. "I'm afraid if I sink any deeper, you'll consume me."

"I want to," she stated, reaching for an olive and popping it inside her mouth. "And I will, if you let me."

She took the knife and cut the baguette. She placed a slice of cheese on top and then brought the morsel to his mouth. "Do you want to taste me?" she whispered seductively, offering him the food. God help him, he took it in and it tasted good.

"I do," he breathed huskily, bringing her to his chest and hugging her close. "I've not a clue what is going on here, but I do want you. From the moment I first saw you there was chemistry between us."

She laughed, patting his knee. "Pure sexual desire, Jason. That's all you feel. It's a natural emotion. A human need."

"It's best if it's not satisfied here. Perhaps you should move out of that cramped staff room, quit the hotel, and come live at my cabin?"

"I'd like that. But I'd be going against the advice of my counselor."

"Forget the counselor," Jason moaned, taking her to the ground, kissing her again, full on the mouth.

Jade grabbed his waist and pulled him closer, her fingers sliding underneath his T-shirt, massaging his back and urging him closer. He groaned when she grasped his lips with her teeth.

"Presently," she cried, her lungs heightening the ache of her pulsing heart, "I'd rather entertain you."

Jason scrutinized the immediate area, but determined they were alone.

"I'll assist with the delivery," Jason groaned, his hands jittery, unbuttoning her jeans, and then finding the metal zipper, slid it downward.

"Oh," she moaned as his hand slipped inside her white denim, "Jason—"

CHAPTER 8

Jason reclined on the armchair inside Ben's office, wondering why his best friend and manager had requested his presence. When Ben had notified him earlier in the day that a situation needed to be resolved, he had refused to disclose the facts over the phone.

He glanced at Ben, placing his hands in his lap, sensing discomfort and consternation in his wrinkled expression. *What was going on?*

"Okay, I'm here. Will you tell me what's wrong?"

"What's gotten into you?" Ben said with a grimace, sitting at his desk and holding the morning paper in his hand. His index finger stabbed at the Harmony Chronicle's front-page headline and the image of a couple kissing passionately. They were vaguely familiar. *Damn it…*

Jason sucked in a breath when he realized that the man and woman in question were none other than Jade and himself. He swore under his breath and heat suffused his cheeks, remembering the passion they had shared a few days ago. Seeing the two of them kissing on the front page of the paper, well, he didn't feel any guilt for having indulged in the embrace, but that ignorant reporter had intruded on their privacy, having the audacity to capture a moment that should have been private, and then publishing it, without their permission? *What a bastard!*

"It was only a bit of kissing and grinding," Jason admitted, embarrassed by the situation.

"That's obvious, but in the open for the townsfolk to see?"

He shook his head, hardly knowing what to say. "Ben, I don't know what business this is of yours; I'm not a child of ten and Jade and I were two consenting adults. We were alone, or at least we thought we were alone."

"I wasn't about to bring up your age, but given that you're thirty, you should have known better and controlled your urges because look at the consequences...You were set on by an interloper. The Harmony Chronicle's reporter, Aaron Bridges, captured a compromising photo."

"So what!" Jason blasted, rising from the chair. He began pacing in front of Ben's desk. "As you say, I'm thirty years old and free to have relations with any woman that I choose."

"Sure, but in the open with the whole world wide web to see? There's enough noise on social media," Ben stated, throwing the paper on his desk. "Aaron mentioned your name in the article, alerting the media to the hotel. It's an embarrassment."

"Hey, no one committed a crime. The image only shows two consenting adults kissing, nothing more. And anyway, who cares about kissing and grinding in our insignificant town?"

"Who cares? I care!" Ben emphasized, clearly rankled. "Have you seen the media trucks, or the photographers with their zoom cameras outside the Thurston this morning? I don't care about the outward show of Jade Carter, country music star. She can sleep with anyone she wants to as long as her exploits don't create an inconvenience for our guests. This state of affairs is partly your fault. What do you intend to do about it?"

Jason had to think about Ben's comment for a moment. A fool would have noticed the commotion surrounding the hotel this morning, but what could he do about the situation after the fact? He couldn't change the past anymore than he could make the problem go away. He'd have to talk to Jade. She had been through this type of viral attention before, maybe she would have a solution.

"This is as sudden a situation for me as it is for you, my friend. I honestly don't know what to do. Maybe Jade will know."

"I've asked Poppy Ellis to keep our starlet on the third floor, cleaning the guest rooms until we can come up with a solution to the problem."

Jason groaned. "I'm sorry, Ben."

Ben raised his hand and flicked it to the side as if the trouble could be swept away as easily. "You'll be further upset when you learn what Mrs. A. has to say about the matter."

Jason studied Ben's earnest expression, worrying. "Mrs. A. knows? I'm almost frightened to hear what she thinks."

"You should be." Ben paused, drumming his fingers on the desk. "Mrs. A. has traditional values. She reads the Harmony Chronicle every week. She's seen the picture in the paper and believes you've compromised a woman's reputation. As far as she's concerned, you should get down on your knees and make amends."

Jason stretched forward, anxiety rising in his chest, his hands suddenly sweaty on his jeans. "What does she mean by that?"

Sighing, Ben stood. His line of vision was direct and serious.

"You better sit for this. She wants you to propose marriage to the singer. Tonight."

"What?" Jason said sarcastically, running his fingers through his hair. He sat on the armchair, again. "You can't be serious. Propose marriage? That's ludicrous! I've only just met the woman."

In shock, Jason didn't know what to say as he watched Ben step from behind his desk and take a chair opposite him. He placed a round metal object in the palm of his hand.

"She's been bold enough to provide this ring for you to use. Mrs. A. feels there's a direct benefit to the hotel, confiding with me that the best part of the deal might be that a Patsy Cline sound-a-like could redeem her reputation, and her career, by singing at the hotel almost every night. She's excited about the possibilities, and you know how she enjoys helping people."

Jason felt the ring in his hand and he understood the weight of the metal and the significance of the band. He was attracted to Jade Carter, but he certainly wasn't ready to put a ring on her finger.

"Oh, no," Jason complained, understanding that Mrs. A. could not be stopped once an idea came to her. He was already assisting her in the search for Emily's lost daughter and the senior was a force to be reckoned with in most situations. He suspected beneath this entire conspiracy that Mrs. A. had a different motive. She liked Jade Carter. Who wouldn't like a woman who sounded like her favorite country star, Patsy Cline!

"Oh yes," Ben supplied, chuckling, shaking his head, for some reason suddenly finding the situation comical. "She expects you to do the deed tonight."

"I had hoped to two days ago," Jason countered mindlessly,

rolling his eyes. "Somehow, I found the strength to fight off my urges."

"We're not talking about sex."

"I know precisely what we're talking about," Jason growled, glancing at the ring. "I need time to think this situation through, to at least help you solve the media problem. But come on already, a man doesn't propose marriage to a woman because of a little foreplay."

"Mrs. A. would beg to differ. Look, I understand how you feel, but I need the media gone, like yesterday. If you have a better solution, you have my attention. Meanwhile, I've had Gill move Jade's belongings to room 32. I don't think it would further the hotel's cause to have a famous star living in the basement."

"Wait a minute. There's no story here and furthermore, I have not agreed to this farce of a plan."

"I suppose we could ask Jade to leave the hotel, but given her financial circumstances, I'm not sure that's a possibility, unless of course 'you' support your country star. You know, buy her a tank of gas and send her back to Vancouver."

"I don't think so," Jason replied, mulling the suggestion over. "There's an attraction between us. I need more time to see if there's anything more."

Ben shook his head. "I've heard you out, Jason. But you created the problem so you have to solve it. One way or another, make those media trucks go away!"

"I'll think about it, but I won't make any promises."

"Think fast. Keep the ruby ring until your decision is final."

EVERY GUEST STAYING at the hotel received a copy of the Harmony Chronicle, and given the front-page image, it didn't take long for Jade to discover the news. Sitting on a bed in a hotel guest room, she cringed, her breath catching in her throat while reading the headline of the local newspaper: *Pick-Necking in the Park.*

"Oh, no," Jade murmured, staring at the image of Jason and herself sharing an intimate moment. She hung her head in shame for not having had more restraint. She dropped the newspaper to her lap. *Why did these image captures always happen to her?* Yet another picture circulating on social media to further depress her career. She didn't need bad press to dampen a career already sinking. *What if Dixon Reed saw the photo?* She knew what he'd think.

Jade Carter hasn't wasted any time digging herself a new den of trouble.

Poppy was pushing the vacuum across the carpet and must have noticed her dazed expression. She turned the noisy beast off and then stepped closer. "Is something wrong?"

Jade was too embarrassed to talk about the truth let alone the journalistic accounting of her behavior, so she picked up the paper and handed it to Poppy. She supposed her Aussie friend didn't see the same unpleasantness as her response was positive. She pointed a finger at the image, grinning. "Is that Jason? Jason the bartender?"

"That's him," Jade replied, sighing, "and me, in the throes of passion."

"Wow!" Poppy chuckled. "I didn't know that Jason had such magnificence hiding under his black cotton shirts."

Poppy joined her on the queen-sized bed, and Jade glanced

at the image again, remembering. "He packs a fine pair of pectoral muscles, too."

She looked pointedly at Jade, her expression rapt. "It's a picture. Don't look so upset."

Jade sighed, took the newspaper back, folded it to hide her shame and then laid it on her lap. "A picture that screams a thousand words of hurt. Will I ever learn from my past mistakes?"

"Jade, if not for the picture, would you second-guess yourself?"

Jade considered Poppy's question, remembering the passionate moments she had shared with Jason. She didn't regret their kisses. Why should she? "Honestly," she admitted, "I don't regret kissing Jason."

"Well, then?" Poppy giggled, taking the paper from her hand and throwing it. "That waste bin is where your hurtful memories belong. Don't worry about it. Focus on the positive. Tell me— how does he kiss? Every woman in this hotel wants a piece of those lips and from what I saw, you were enjoying the encounter."

"Whatever I was feeling then," Jade remarked, recalling that he was a good kisser, "it's not proper to discuss. I can't believe this happened. Awful news media, they enjoy capturing a fall from grace, and now that there's a new story to tempt a viewer's imagination, I won't be left alone."

"So what," Poppy bantered, attempting to support her new friend. "Let the media play their games and capture their moments. You seemed happy in that photo. I saw the expression on your face as you studied that picture of you and Jason. You were smiling."

Jade smirked slightly, but glanced downwards. "I admit it;

we shared an immediate connection. I've never taken such a risk with a man. My goodness, Poppy, we've only just met."

"How old are you? Twenty-something? Close to thirty?" Poppy probed. "As we Aussies say, an adult woman doesn't need permission to be with a man."

"I know what the article suggests, but the lower part of the picture has been blurred out on purpose, to suggest sensual behavior. We never had sex!"

Poppy retrieved the paper and pointed at the image again, grinning like a cheshire cat. "You sure look close to it."

Jade shook her head, trying to quell her anxiety. "Well, one of us had some restraint, *gratefully*, or a different portrait of an affair would have been published on this page. With a big black 'X' highlighting the portion too risqué to publish."

Poppy rose from the bed, her expression thoughtful. "You've been through a difficult time, or at least this is what you've shared with me. Maybe you could turn this story around to benefit your career?"

"What are you suggesting? I see the thoughts turning in your head."

"I'm thinking if Jason is game to the strategy, use him to add interest to your career. He's not a fling. You're in love, or something like that. You met him long before the day in the park and you've kept your love affair a secret! The cameras will eat it up."

"The photogs have already had their fun and I wouldn't do that to a man," Jade confessed. "Anyway, when I do welcome a man into my life, I want him to be all in. I've been hurt before."

Poppy grabbed the vacuum. "I saw the way you were looking at him. You were all in. Something has already been turned on."

Poppy switched the vacuum on as if to make a statement

and began removing the crumbs from the rug with a pointed look. Jade wished she could clean away the trouble from her life as easily. Rising from the bed, she reached for the duster and joined her friend in their work.

When Jason entered the guest room, they stopped cleaning. The serious expression etched on his face, mirrored her own guilt and anxiety.

"Jade, we need to talk. Poppy, can you give us some privacy?"

"Of course." Poppy grinned, turning the vacuum off. "I'll be in the staff room if you need me," she said, winking at Jade, then leaving the room.

Jade kept dusting, refusing to look at the subject of her weakness. "You saw the article?"

"I'm sorry," Jason offered, walking toward her. "Can you ever forgive me? Hell, I don't know why I acted like that. It's too late to change anything, but I know I should have had more restraint."

"Yes, you should have." Jade paused, recalling their heated kisses, shaking her head. "But I should have been more cautious than you. I confess it, I was attracted to you, an attraction that only matured when you took me to that romantic spot near the creek."

"It's a beautiful place," Jason said with a half smile, stepping closer.

"Yes, it was." Jade blushed, her cheeks suffusing with color. "But I should have had some self-control. I know how the media hounds me. This situation is my fault, my misery and my miss-calculation. I seem to make these mistakes over and over again."

She saw that Jason was gazing at her with some seriousness. "Don't be so hard on yourself, the attraction was mutual, but I usually have more restraint, too. I'm sorry. I felt like a bee drawn to the nectar inside a pretty flower. Too bright, too beautiful and sweet-tasting, to stay away."

"Let me assure you, I didn't mind at all." Jade giggled, clasping the duster to her chest. "And if not for the image in the paper, I'd have no regrets. I'd even request a second date, but what do we do now?"

"I'd like to put the picture business behind us to contemplate the prospects of the future, but the media attention is causing problems for the hotel. Ben and Mrs. A. think they've found the perfect solution to the problem."

"I remember Ben, but who is Mrs. A? Surely, not your mother?"

"No, not my mother," Jason replied, his hand sliding through his black hair. "Although, I wouldn't mind so much if she was my mother. Madeline Arbuckle is a wealthy matron and a longtime resident of the hotel. She's been kind to me and her opinions carry some weight."

"I can't begin to understand why our situation should matter to a resident living at the hotel?"

"Don't let me give you the impression that she's just any resident. Known as Mrs. A., she's an important matriarch of The Thurston Hotel. What she says goes."

"I assume she's aware of the article in the paper?"

"Very much so, I'm afraid. She reads the Harmony Chronicle every week."

"All right," Jade muttered. "I'll presume that Mrs. Arbuckle's opinions are important. What does she think should happen to rectify this problem?"

Jason pulled a band of gold from his pocket. He gazed at the ring and rolled it between his fingers. "She says… I have compromised you. She thinks I should…"

Jade stepped closer and scrutinized the object in his hand. "What do you have there, Jason?"

"A ring." He sighed, his voice soft and low. "It belongs to Mrs. A."

"Jason," Jade exclaimed, wondering what this meant. "Surely you're not thinking about something as ludicrous as proposing?"

"Ben and Mrs. A. say that I need to make amends."

"Amends?" Jade said with surprise, stepping forward, her strident tone expressing her sarcasm. "That's ridiculous. You've done nothing wrong."

"If I asked, what would you say?"

His comment caught her by surprise. *What would she say?* "I'd say…"

Jade stared at his concerned expression, wondering what he was thinking. And she thought of Poppy's advice and wondered how this turn of events could benefit her career. No, such considerations were wrong. She wouldn't do it to him. She wouldn't do it to herself.

"No," she said, shaking her head, "I'd have to say no."

Jason didn't reply right away. Jade wondered what his silence meant. Scrutinizing the floor, he placed the ring back inside his pocket. "Then, how do we get rid of the paparazzi parked outside the hotel?"

Jade walked to the window, pulled aside the draperies and looked out. "Oh no," she whispered, dropping the feather duster on the floor. "The bloodhounds have arrived."

Permitting the draperies to slide back into place, she approached Jason. "I can't afford more bad press. Normally, I wouldn't entertain a dramatic ploy such as a marriage proposal, but this image could really hurt my career. Are you sure about this?"

"No," he whispered, pulling the ring from inside his pocket again. "I'm not sure of anything. Maybe we can fake an engagement. Breaking off the commitment—later—is a plausible possibility. Relationships end all the time."

He reached forward and grabbed her hand. Jade didn't stop him. Astonished, she watched the bartender slip the ring—five rubies set in a band of gold—on her ring finger. "Would you look at that," he murmured, obviously surprised, "It fits. I'm not asking you to marry me, Jade. If we go through with this pretense, the engagement would be for show."

"I understand," she said, the emotion welling in her chest.

"So, what do you think, should we go through with it?"

"I'm a willing participant." Jade made known, gazing at the stunning ring. She liked the band circling her ring finger. She had always wanted such a commitment. "It will match my stage outfits," she offered without thinking.

"Oh and by the way, Gill has moved your luggage to room 32. And from now on, you're only to sing, no more attending to guest rooms in the hotel. Ben says working as a maid would hinder our story."

Jade studied the ring. "What happens next?"

"I'll ask you for a commitment of sorts in front of the audience tonight. You'll be excited. You'll say yes."

"I'd better give this back to you then, you'll need it when you kneel down." Jade took the ring off and placed it on his palm. "You don't have to do this. It won't make the rat pack go away. I know from experience, their interest will only grow."

"Yes, I know. Dogs will be dogs. But the story might end sooner, and hopefully, disappear faster."

"I don't know what to say, Jason. You're taking a great risk for my reputation."

He stepped forward; he cupped her cheeks, staring deeply into her eyes. "Don't worry. I'm not the kind of man to ever *let you down easy*. I'm firm in my decisions."

He spoke the lyrics of her song almost too easily. She turned away from him, feeling ashamed, but he wouldn't permit her to shirk his attention and urged her back to his serious expression.

"There's one more thing. Tonight, after your set is finished, I'm taking my fiancée home. I feel it's the only solution to removing the cameras from the hotel. Does this concern you?"

"Jason?" she gasped, appealing to him with outstretched hands. "It's not very proper."

He grinned, then pulled her into his embrace. She rested against his chest, grateful for his support. His hand climbed the back of her neck and lingered in her hair. His lingering touch felt good.

"Neither was a romp beside the creek. It's either come home with me or leave the hotel. But don't worry because I won't take advantage of you. You'll simply be my guest, and I know you need the work from the Hamilton wedding."

Jade nodded in resignation. "I'll come home with you."

Soon after he left the guest room, she collapsed to the bed, acknowledging that her future was completely out of her control. She didn't know why the tears started to fall, as she finally had a man in her life who was not only willing to support her, but stand by her in a time of need.

She gazed at her naked finger, knowing the promise that would soon surround it. In her opinion, no other man had acted so bravely. Jason was a true *knight* in shining armor. A gentleman living in the modern age.

CHAPTER 9

The Thomas Lounge was reaching its guest capacity. Already on stage, Jade had been watching members of the audience entering the lounge with a mounting curiosity. Hotel staff, townsfolk, media, and one intrepid reporter, Aaron Bridges, had been wandering through the dining space for the past fifteen minutes, every one of them searching for a place to sit at a table, or failing that, a seat at the bar. In response to the great turnout, the hotel management had begun placing extra chairs along the perimeters of the lounge as well as in the lobby area where guests would have a limited view at best.

Jade was shocked beyond words. Were these patrons really here to see the one and only… *Jade Carter?*

She studied the commotion, listening to the buzz of conversation while making final tuning adjustments to her guitar. She glanced at her fingers, plucking the guitar strings, trying to hear musical tones above the din, but despite the noise and media attention, her heart was singing, swelling inside her chest; as a proposal was foremost on her mind.

Most women had no idea when their significant other would

propose. Jade had always hoped for such a tender moment, when the love of her life would kneel, take her hand into his own, and ask her the all-important question: *Will you marry me?*

She sighed, picturing the drama… Jason kneeling in full view of the audience. How would she respond to his question? Would she accept his proposal? *Saying, yes?*

Jason was here, too, tending the bar. She glanced across a sea of people, seeking his attention. He returned her stare. When he nodded his head and winked, she understood that desire may have lit his knowing expression. My goodness, she considered, her cheeks blushing pink, the man's going to do it. He's going to propose! Jason Knight, who she had only just met, was about to propose a *fake* marriage to Jade Carter.

Anxiety danced in her stomach as she thought about her set and the show. Her conscience warred with the knowledge, *what are you doing?* But the fierce part of her personality that appreciated the value of commitment, looked forward to delighting the audience, and it seemed like the show was about to begin.

She watched Ben Thurston approach a second mic and take the silver length in his hands. He began the introductions. "We have quite a crowd here tonight. I don't think I have ever seen so many people packed inside this lounge," he said with a grin, winking at the star attraction. "Myself and the entire Thurston family are delighted to have you join us, to welcome an award-winning country music star to the hotel. All the way from Vancouver, The Thurston Hotel is proud to welcome, Jade Carter. Please give her a warm round of applause."

Jade smiled, expressing her gratitude, and then waited for the hand-clapping to quiet. When the audience was ready, she spoke into the silver microphone. "Thank you for the warm welcome, Mr. Thurston," she responded, appraising the crowded room. She sought the woman who had been kind, having offered a ring that must have been expensive. Not many people were that selfless.

"There's a special guest in the audience tonight who has requested songs by the one and only Patsy Cline. Mrs. Arbuckle, this night and the songs I'm about to sing, are dedicated to you."

Mrs. A. smiled and the audience clapped in response to the announcement, but when Jade began strumming her guitar, the noise diminished to silence. Jade winked at Mrs. A. and nodded at Roberta Smythe, who sat beside her two little girls, Reba and Dolly.

Jade opened the set with the song *Strange*, as she thought the lyrics were appropriate for the upcoming drama. She smiled in the direction of Jason as she sang: *I guess that I was just your puppet, you held on a string...* but look what thoughts can bring... How strange.

She followed that storied version with *Crazy*, *Walkin' after Midnight* and *Leavin' on your mind*.

As she sang the last few lyrics, she gazed at Jason, seeing only him. *"If you have leaving on your mind, hurt me now, get it over."*

But Jason remained at his post tending the bar. He wasn't leaving. She continued singing through the entire set. Taking a deep breath at the end, she decided to brave out the act with the song, *True Love*.

She spoke into the mic. "Finding love is not easy for most people. But with certain risks, possibilities for love can be realized. Jason Knight, I'd like to dedicate this song to you."

Sitting beneath the raised platform, Mrs. A. smiled and

Roberta's eyebrows rose upward. Everyone who knew the bartender stared at him as Jade began strumming. Jason Knight's attention was solely on her. He simply smiled as if he was enjoying the drama.

Jade couldn't bear to even glance in the man's direction as she took this moment seriously. She was nervous, afraid her voice would break. After all, Jason was assuming a great risk for her.

"True Love, by Patsy Cline." She breathed throatily into the mic.

Jade closed her eyes, humming *True Love*, bathing her soul with the music and preparing for the final act to come. When she opened her eyes, Jason was walking toward her. She watched him as he strode closer, singing the final lyrical line.

> "But I'll give to you,
> if you'll give to me,
> A love that's forever true…"

Jason soon held the microphone that Ben had spoken into earlier. "Jade Carter," he breathed throatily, "I know we've only just met, but you've captured my heart with a love forever true. Will you do me the honor of capturing your love as well?"

She watched him where he stood at the microphone stand, astonished to hear his question, even though she had known this moment would arrive.

This was crazy.

A nervous giggle escaped her lips as she spoke into the mic, her lips rising into a semblance of a smile. It wasn't really a proposal.

"But, Jason," she teased, sighing, "we've only just met."

"Have you got leaving on your mind, Ms. Carter?"

"Not that, Mr. Knight. I'm a puppet for your love. There might be strings attached, in time, but I'm saying yes."

The audience rose to their feet, clapping and roaring aloud with their applause. Someone whistled. People loved this kind of show and Jade wouldn't disappoint them by making it known that this was a well-thought-out act, an enacted drama played out for the benefit of the cameras. It wasn't real.

Still, she wished it was true, *true love* that is.

Jade let her guitar slide to the ground, oblivious of the plucking sound, given she was in a hurry to reach her pretend groom. Jason extended his arms and pulled her into his embrace, kissing her mouth and devouring her lips. Her knees suddenly felt weak. The tender moment caused the audience to clap even louder. For an act, it sure felt real.

"That's all for tonight, folks." Jason chuckled into the mic. "I'm taking my country star home, far away from the lights of The Thurston Hotel. Good evening and thanks for coming."

Jade stifled a giggle when Jason lifted her into his arms and carried her away from the Thomas Lounge. He passed through a line of assembled guests, taking her across the foyer and straight through the lobby in his mission to reach the front doors.

She was at ease in his arms. A girl could get lost in his strength, his muscular arms. Everyone needed someone to hold, someone to love, and she was no different. She laid her arm across his shoulders, feeling his strength, wishing this situation was real.

"You can put me down, Jason. The show is over."

"Not on your life," he chortled, squeezing her thigh. "You said yes. You're coming with me."

"I'm coming with you? Where are you taking me?"

"I told you earlier, I thought the only way to fend off the media hounds was to get you away from the hotel. So I'm taking you home."

"Is that so?" She frowned, second-guessing her previous decision. Was she really letting this happen? She was actually entertaining leaving the hotel to retreat to a complete stranger's house? Now, that was true fodder for a newshound's imagination.

"Hey, it's not a perfect situation, but you'll be more comfortable. We're about to exit the hotel. Are you ready?"

Jade took a deep breath. "I'm ready."

"Well, look happy about it, darling. The camera lens waits for her star. The show isn't over yet."

As they came outside the Thurston's front doors, the night lit up with white camera-flashes. Jade smiled at the group of photographers, while nuzzling closer to Jason's neck. She knew how to act. She'd donned that owl look, sighting the camera lens many times before with her lips a pretty pout.

Gill Landis opened the door of an older, gold truck and Jason placed her on the passenger's seat. She missed the scent of his leather musk at their separation, but he was soon entering the truck through the driver's door, taking his seat and turning the key in the ignition. The truck sparked to life.

"Are you really taking me to your place?"

He flashed her a sensual grin as he peeled away from the curb. "You're in my Ford, Jade, and I can't wait to get you home!"

"You didn't put the ring on my finger." She giggled nervously, wondering why.

"I'm still thinking about that part of the show." He grinned, tapping his fingers against the steering wheel. "Not quite ready to take that all-important step. Not yet."

"You're not a risk-taker, then."

"I didn't say that."

"That's okay, you don't have to say anything. I'm fine with this act progressing at a normal pace. But don't fool yourself, there's a relationship developing here. And I don't mind it, not one bit. Oh, and Jason?"

"Yes, darling?"

"No man's ever taken such a risk for me. How can I thank you for protecting my reputation?"

Jason scrutinized her with a cheerful yet desirous mien. He surprised her when he winked. His upturned lips and sensual body language suggested what their conversation could not hide.

Undeterred, Jade grinned in response, her cheeks heating, seeing he was a man like any other and she didn't mind at all.

JADE LISTENED to the hum of the engine as they drove along the Trans-Canada highway. Night had fallen. Only the glow of the headlights captured the road ahead. Jade couldn't tell where they were going.

"Where do you live, Jason?"

He kept his hands on the wheel and his attention on the road ahead, so Jade could study him freely while waiting for him to respond. She liked what she saw.

"Southeast of Harmony, a private getaway where nothing but peace and solitude can find us."

"I like the sound of that," Jade mused. "A home where a

camera lens can't intrude on a person's private life. Tell me about it."

He gave her a sidelong glance before returning his attention to driving. "It won't be the luxury you're accustomed to. I built a log cabin in the woods with tall spruce surrounding the structure. It has one hell of a mountain view. A simple home with a patchwork quilt on the bed. I'm sure you'll find it comfortable."

She contemplated his statement as he turned south down a secondary highway. "Do you have neighbors?"

"Not even one, not close to me anyway. We will have complete privacy. Free to do whatever we want. No camera lens to disturb us this time."

Suddenly shy, Jade gripped her lip with her teeth and looked outside the truck window, grateful he couldn't see the color flaming her cheeks as she thought about what could happen between them at his cabin. "Do you like your privacy?"

"I prefer the peace and quiet. I used to live in Calgary. My life was busier then."

Jade studied Jason. "Have you always been a bartender?"

"Not always."

"What did you do before?"

"I had my own business, managing a consulting firm. It was quite successful."

"Why did you leave, if you don't mind me asking?"

He grew silent. Jade pondered the hum of the motor, contemplated his fingers massaging the steering wheel, his attention focused on the road ahead and the sudden curve in the roadway.

Finally, he sighed. "I had a heart attack. It was either keep living life full throttle, my life filled with constant job stress, or start a new adventure."

"You're so young. You appear fit, strong. You can't be more than thirty? I'm so sorry to hear that."

"You don't have to be old to have a heart attack. It caught me by surprise."

"And how did you end up working at The Thurston Hotel, tending bar?"

"That?" He glanced at her, grinning. "Ben needed help and we're good friends. I remember telling him: *just this one night.* But one night turned into a few more. Ben and I go back a long way; we're childhood buddies. And why not work at the hotel, it gets me out of the house."

"Do you enjoy tending bar?"

"I meet lots of people and hear even more stories," he commented, chuckling. "If I hadn't made that decision, I wouldn't have met you."

"Are you glad you met me?"

"Time will tell."

They were quiet for the rest of the journey to the cabin. Jade kept her questions to herself while gazing beyond the window, contemplating the passing spruce and leafy poplar trees. She didn't know what she was searching for in the night shadows. She had to admit that this situation had her a bit nervous.

Sure, Jason seemed like a kind man, but she had just met him. And here she was traveling to his home, alone inside his purring truck. A strange prospect for a woman.

At length they arrived at the cabin, and Jason stopped the truck on the front driveway. As the headlights illuminated the log structure, she considered how manly the cabin appeared, until Jason interrupted her thoughts.

"We're not that happy-go-lucky couple about to get married, but if it makes you happy, I'll carry you across the threshold."

"Would you?" She grinned, giggling. "I'd like to experience a happily-ever-after and lasting kind of ending. Every woman wants her dreams to come true."

"I aim to make your dreams come true all right, Jade Carter."

Jade smacked him against the arm. "Jason Knight, you say that as if you have ulterior motives."

"Trying to keep you satisfied, ma'am," he exclaimed, exiting the truck and closing the door. She pivoted to the window and waited for Jason on the passenger seat, sitting there like a nervous schoolgirl while he retrieved her suitcases from the truck box, and then took them inside the cabin. He returned and opened her door.

She searched the light in his amber eyes as he paused, taking her in. She swung her legs over the lip of the vehicle's edge and almost slid off the seat, still wearing her flashy red dress with matching high heels. "You don't have to carry me. I know this stage show is no more than a theatrical performance."

He reached forward, grasped her hand, and pulled her close to his chest as if they were at a dance and he'd just taken her as his partner. "Does it feel like a drama?" he asked, swinging her close to his chest, his hand suddenly warming the small of her back. "Some parts of this newness feel all too real."

"Which part?" Jade asked, blushing, but feeling bold leaning against his chest, so close to his neck she breathed the woodsy scent of his cologne before he confidently swept her into his arms. She giggled, hearing her own laughter bubble from her lips as he carried her across the gravel driveway, pausing at the threshold of his home.

"This part," he whispered in her ear, stepping through the archway of the door. Once through, he nudged the door shut with his booted foot.

He paused against the door, still holding her, not putting her down. She couldn't escape from the heat she glimpsed in his eyes. "I'd like to take you somewhere."

Jade breathed deeply. "Where would that be? You've only just carried me across the threshold."

"My bed," he responded too quickly. "Your teasing has me fired up."

"I'm not sure the next step in our relationship should happen so fast."

"Are you turning modest on me now?"

"Look, Jason," Jade began, sighing, but her heart pulsed with excitement. "It wouldn't be right to climb into bed with you. I need some time."

Growling playfully, he carried her across the floor of the cabin, and she pondered the ceiling logs until they reached a rustic couch. But he refused to release her from his embrace and they collapsed together on the couch. As she sat on his lap, Jason scrutinized her eyes and for the life of her she couldn't retreat from his or her need.

"I've learned that time is a fleeting thing," Jason admitted. "Since my heart attack, I live my life by embracing what I have before it dies away."

Jade had heard a dozen excuses as to why she should succumb to passion, so this reason wasn't new. "Are you saying," Jade paused, momentarily glancing away, "that I should accept some risk?"

She didn't shift away when his lips brushed across her mouth, tasting her lips, stoking that sensitive spot in her gut.

Being held in his warm embrace with his hand seductively massaging her arm. Well, this wooing compelled her toward temptation, but she'd be risking further destruction of her soul. To play at love on a grassy knoll was one thing, to climb into his heated bed to lose herself to deeper passions, quite another. Despite what he thought, she wasn't that type of girl.

"Are you sure?" he asked, stroking her arm.

"I'm sure," Jade whispered, kissing him back, thinking she should push him away, but she tugged him closer instead, almost begging for another touch.

"Look," Jade gasped, her breathing quickening, "I appreciate your kindness and generosity, and there's nothing more I want right now than to join you in your bedroom. But I must not submit to temptation."

He gently touched her cheek and rested his forehead against hers. "Why not? I promise you, I'd not disappoint."

Jade quivered with excitement; his fingers explored the soft tissues of her neck, drifted inside her dress and played with her bra strap.

She gasped. The flutter of her breath matched her heartbeat. "I'm in trouble here," Jade breathed heavily, pulling Jason closer, squirming in his lap, grasping his emerald-green tie and pulling him nearer to her lips.

"What are you asking me to do, darling?"

She reached for his hand and paused momentarily when she held it above her heart, but then taking a shuddering breath, placed his hand inside her bra to grasp her left breast.

She considered giving in to his quest; she searched for a reason to abort their seduction. To say no… "What if you have another heart attack?"

"I'll die a happy man," he breathed against her lips, kissing her.

She returned his kiss, sighing as he stroked the soft tissues of her breast, her inner oven burning with need. "Oh, my," she moaned.

"Darling," he whispered in her ear, "pleasure awaits you, if you say yes."

"Jason," Jade mumbled, "you've made your point quite clear. Take me to your castle. To hell with convictions, too. I need the love you want to give me."

JASON LIFTED Jade in his arms and carried her from the living area to his rustic bedroom. She reclined against his chest, staring at him with an expression of wonder. As he placed her on the patchwork quilt of his bed, he asked himself: *what was she thinking?*

When he leaned over her, taking the liberty to ponder her beautiful face, she clearly contemplated the masculine arms resting on either side of her shoulders.

"What are you searching for?" she asked, taking a tiny quivering breath. "What do you see when you study me with such devotion?"

"You're beautiful," he replied, licking his lips. "I want you to know that I take my relationships seriously, and I don't bring just anyone to this place. I have not been with another woman in a long time. I promise to respect your wishes and I'll be… gentle."

She reached to him and touched his grizzled cheek. He liked her fingers on his face. "I like the passion, the kindness I see in your eyes." She moved over and made a space for him. She had yet to remove her heels.

"Are you sure, Jason Knight? It's not too soon for us to show some restraint."

"I've brought you to my castle. I want to treat you like a queen. And… I want to make love to you, Jade Carter. If you'll have me."

She grasped the waistband of his denim jeans, pulled him closer, then undid the silver button. Her fingers quivering as if her experience lacked. She eased the zipper downward and his indrawn breath didn't escape her notice. Then, she helped him lower his pants to the floor. He laid down beside her and she seemed comfortable with him lying near.

"I want to love you, too, Jason Knight, and I hope I don't regret this come morning."

CHAPTER 10

When Jade awoke the next morning, sunlight was streaming through the windowpanes, but the light was nothing in comparison to the man lying beside her. Warm beneath a patchwork quilt, she was acutely aware of Jason's proximity with his groin nestled close to her bottom. His arm rested on her waist and his fingers dangled near her belly, stimulating awareness and desire.

Recognition and regret. Weakened by her own needs, she'd acted on impulse, yielding to passion. She'd satisfied two sexual appetites and enjoyed every minute of their love-making, however, rule number one in the goal of overcoming addictive tendencies had been broken.

Who she allowed into her life—

Now, the cravings for more would begin.

Jason appeared to be a good man, a *hot damn* specimen of the opposite sex and she was attracted to his virility. It felt good having him near her, but what she really desired was love, but sweetheart connections didn't happen this fast.

Though Jade was comfortable lying beside Jason, she left his warmth, only to stand before his sleeping form to study his handsome and rugged face. She wrapped her arms around herself, shivering, reflecting on the cold air numbing her skin as butterflies fluttered inside her stomach, alerting her passions simply by staring at his sleeping face.

Should she get back in the bed? She wanted to return to his sheets, if only to rouse him in order to feel his fingers massaging her skin like the night before, so his sensual pleasure might make her warm and tingly, all over again!

Jade, what are you thinking? Quit tempting fate!

Sighing, she retreated from his attraction and entered the ensuite, attended to her needs, and then pulled on a robe hanging from a hook on the door.

She paused where she stood, leaning against the wooden frame, her fingers stroking soft navy fibers while smelling the masculine musk the robe gave off. *Jason—*

She left the ensuite but paused to study Jason. He stretched in his sleep, revealing his chest and a nest of dark hair curling between his nipples. She sighed, perusing his handsome face. Why she hoped he might notice that his bed contained one less person, she couldn't say. A part of her hungered for *love* so profoundly, it was nice to hope a man might miss her presence, and want more from her than a quick tumble beneath his sheets. *Why was she so weak?* She had given in, had given too much of herself away.

She left the master suite and walked to the kitchen. Adjoining the living room, the space formed a comfortable great room. She found the coffee maker and prepared a pot to brew. Coffee was a needed drug this early in the morning. She couldn't start her day without a cup.

She waited patiently for the dripping to stop while studying the living area. The kitchen was spotless. The black granite counter glistened and every dish, cloth, and container was neatly organized and put away. No soiled dishes had been left inside the sink. Impressive, considering Jason likely maintained the cabin by himself, unlike a country music star who employed a maid, or rather, had employed a maid.

Jade ruminated how her life might be changing for the better, but she put the feeling aside when the scent of coffee filled the air. She poured herself a cup, then holding the warm mug in her hands, walked beyond the kitchen to consider the rest of the living space.

She had never stayed in a log cabin before and thought the room seemed homey and welcoming. Long logs formed the walls, and between expansive windows, an impressive stone fireplace rose to the ceiling. A rust-colored area rug had been placed in front of the couch; the place where Jason had embraced her the night before. Sweet memories stirred. Trying to escape the sudden guilt, she left the great room, approached the patio door and grasped the handle. Passing through the doorway, she took in the environment outside the cabin; a covered deck, and a beautiful and serene mountain landscape.

Taking a sip of coffee, she reclined to a nearby lounge chair and quietly contemplated the bright sunlight streaming through a landscape thick with spruce, while enjoying the birds twittering in the trees. A tiny chipmunk scampered across the ground close to the deck. She smiled, laughed, watching the small animal prance across the lawn with its flicking tail. She closed her eyes, breathing the clean and fresh mountain air, a cool balm scented with pine that could only bring goodness inside her lungs.

Sipping coffee, she curled up on the log lounge chair and

tucked her bare feet underneath the robe. When the door slid wide and Jason stepped onto the deck, wearing only his jockeys and carrying a cup of coffee, she smiled at him, giggling again, taking in his appearance.

He grinned back in response. "If you come outside dressed like that, you're sure to catch a cold."

He stepped toward her, amusement creasing his cheeks. His fingers found the edges of the bathrobe then slid along the open neckline, causing her flesh to tingle. "I'd be wearing something else entirely," he whispered, kissing her lips. "But a wood sprite seems to have borrowed my robe."

"It was the nearest piece of clothing at hand. What could I do? My clothing is still packed."

"Except for what you left on the floor. We'll have to rectify that situation. I tell you what, I'll make a space for your clothing, and for you, too."

"Will you? Will you make room for me?"

"Hey," Jason muttered, assisting her to her feet. "I would have thought that a bestselling country music star would have more confidence in herself."

"I appreciate your offer. It's generous, but I don't expect you to change your life for me. I know this situation is temporary. My concern doesn't come from a lack of confidence. There's no end of bachelor opportunities, I'm afraid. But it's difficult finding a lasting relationship when most partners only want what your money can gain them. I've found that most men don't see the real me, and aren't willing to make a sincere space in their lives."

"A woman as pretty as you? There will always be greedy men who want nothing but the material, but life is built on more than money and sex. Jade, I'm willing to make sincere changes for you, even if the accommodations are only temporary."

Jade followed Jason back inside the cabin. Closing the door, he led her to the kitchen table where he offered her a chair. "Money speaks volumes. But now that my cash flow is slim to none, maybe we're on a more equal footing."

Jason grinned; he knelt before her, pressing close with his hand on the table, giving her a contemplative view of grizzled cheeks and a muscular chest. "I don't want your money. I'm not that type of man. But I'd be lying if I didn't acknowledge your attributes, definitely assets, which I appreciate having touched them. I'd like to see what more you could offer me."

"Jason," Jade scolded, her face taking on a sterner expression. "You're propositioning me again, and I'm far more than a one-night stand."

"Oh honey," Jason said with a grin, his lips so close, the temptation to kiss him garnered an exquisite sigh. "I'll have you know, you're the passion every man dreams about." His fingers slid across her hand. His lips found her mouth and nibbled at her lip. "If you've come to my cabin fishing for my attention, I've already been lured by your bait and taken your hook. You have my full attention, and while our relationship may have begun with a strong connection, I'm not opposed to seeing if the show could become the lasting harmony you mentioned."

"Oh Jason," Jade sighed, surprised at his kind words. "I've fallen so far. You must know this before you even consider anything more."

"I don't care about your past and I'm not worried about what the papers say. You and I will explore whatever is happening between us. But before we talk further, are you hungry? Can I make you breakfast?"

"What did you have in mind to satisfy, my aw, hunger?"

He grinned, kissing her lips. "None of that, you sweet vixen. We have a full day ahead of us. I'm meeting Ben and Melanie for lunch later this afternoon, and you're meeting Wendy Thurston and Riley Hamilton to talk about the wedding."

"Oh I am, am I? You have our whole day planned out?"

He helped her to stand and then embraced her, hugging her close to his chest. "I don't have everything planned. Not yet. But believe me, I'm thinking about the future."

Jade nestled beneath his chin, close to his chest and even closer to his beating heart. *How had she found this man?* He was too good to be true. She hoped she didn't do anything to mess with this budding relationship.

CHAPTER 11

For the meeting with Riley Hamilton, Jade had chosen casual business attire. She adored the checked blouse, navy pencil skirt, and heeled oxford booties, an ensemble that styled her into the country music star she had once been, and in a minor way, refreshed her self esteem by revealing to the client she would soon meet, the flawless reflection of her richer, former self. The high-fashion apparel hid her weaknesses and failures, making her feel like a million bucks.

Jade reflected on the money she'd wasted due to her addictions. Relying on the goodwill of Jason Knight and Ben Thurston, hurt her pride. She wished she hadn't misused the funds in her bank account. How could she have been so foolish?

But life carried on and no one needed to know her financial status, or her imperfections. Flaws shouldn't be captured by the media. And this meeting, no matter how minor it seemed to be, could be the initiative that helped her recover, revive, and perhaps save her ailing career.

Entering the Foothills Dining Room, Jade searched for the bride in a crowded dining space. When Riley raised her hand

and waved, Jade maneuvered through the tables, grasped a chair, then sat opposite the bride and the hotel's event coordinator.

"Hi, Jade. Thank you for meeting with me." Riley clasped her hands on top of the table, then took a deep breath. "I can't believe you're here, or that you've agreed to sing at my wedding. I'm grateful. And I guess I'd be remiss if I didn't introduce you to the hotel's event coordinator, Wendy Thurston."

"Welcome, Jade. I'm delighted to make your acquaintance."

Jade smiled at Wendy while reflecting on the opulence of the dining room. "Pleased to meet you, too."

Riley touched her hand. "Look at your amazing outfit. Where did you buy it?"

"I honestly don't know," Jade admitted. "When I could afford a stylist, clothing was selected and purchased for me. I'd keep the garments I liked and send the rest back."

"Wow," Riley exclaimed, "that's amazing."

"I hate shopping," Wendy Thurston said, rolling her eyes. "I wish I could afford to hire a stylist to shop for me."

"You should know," Jade began, "I didn't hire a stylist because I don't enjoy shopping. I do. But the media spy on me wherever I go. No one enjoys searching through racks of clothing with the bother of a camera flash, or worse, the worry of a crazed fan causing me harm. It's safer to hire a stylist."

"Harmony may be a small town," Wendy quipped, tapping her pen on the table, "but we're not immune from media attention. We're sad to inform you that Aaron Bridges, Harmony's most annoying reporter…"

"Oh yes," Riley grumbled, her tone curt, "I see he's entered the dining room. Too bad there's still a few tables open."

Jade groaned. "Maybe he won't bother us, but if he does sneak a photo, as you say, I look great."

Suddenly two women approached their table. Jade reflected on their matching black blazers. The uniforms marked the ladies as hotel staff.

"Jade, permit me to introduce Bailey Thurston and Melanie Thurston, my sister and sister-in-law," Wendy informed.

"If it's not too much trouble, we'd like to join you," the woman named Melanie announced.

Suddenly, Jade felt surrounded. Her insides filled with anxiety. She hadn't anticipated this many people at the meeting and two more family members made her feel uncomfortable. "You're welcome to join us, but I'm not here for my own amusements. I'm here to discuss the upcoming wedding with Riley."

The ladies disregarded her comment and pulled a table over as if they were accustomed to living life on their own terms. Bailey sat beside Wendy and Melanie sat on the opposite side, leaving a chair-space between them. Jade was grateful she hadn't sat directly beside her, as the empty chair gave her some room to breathe.

"We don't mean to interrupt your meeting," the curly-haired brunette known as Bailey declared. "The Thurston family wants to show a united front where you're concerned, and Ben and Jason were having lunch together when they noticed that reporter, Aaron Bridges, entering the hotel," Bailey said, pointing. "We don't want you to feel uncomfortable, we're just here to support you and protect you if necessary, and let me tell you, we know how to take care of our own!"

"And Riley, too!" Melanie remarked.

"Well—" Riley said, raising her eyebrows. "While I appreciate your consideration, I can protect myself, however, it's always nice to see you ladies. You're welcome to join us. Oh, no," she hastened to add, "I don't know what's worse, that horrible reporter or my mother. Here she comes to complicate the situation."

"I think it's good to have a positive point of view, Riley, however, maybe we can sic your mother on the reporter." Melanie snickered.

Jade shook her head, reflecting on her weaknesses. She glanced at her water glass, thirsting, feeling like she could drink a whole bottle of pure clean vodka if it were handy. She reached for her glass and took a sip.

"Permit me to introduce my mother, Lilith Hamilton."

"Don't sound so surprised to see me, Riley. When I heard you were meeting Miss Carter, I wanted to see for myself what the sensationalism was about."

"It's nice to meet…"

"Oh, the pleasure is all mine, Jade Carter."

"Here," Wendy interjected, rising from her chair. "You can take my seat beside your daughter."

"Oh, that's all right. I know Riley is not impressed that I'm here. I'll sit at the end of the table where I can be a part of the conversation."

Jade could only watch in surprise when Lilith retrieved a chair from another table of patrons, without even bothering to ask if it was being used. She placed it at the end of the table.

"Okay, Mom. But promise to be nice or I'll have to ask you to leave."

"I'll be nice," Lilith declared, sitting.

Wendy cleared her voice. "Let's get down to business. Jade, I'm not sure if we have formally asked you to sing at Riley's wedding."

"Well, no," Jade replied. "I'm not sure if Riley is aware of the situation that brought me to Harmony, but Roberta, the front desk clerk, sent a fan letter to me with a request to sing. And then when I arrived at the hotel, it was quite a mystery to everyone why I was even here."

"Quite rude of the clerk if you ask me," Lilith commented, "sticking her nose where it doesn't belong."

"I think Roberta's scheme was clever," Melanie responded. "Riley has long been a fan of yours, Jade, and the letter did achieve its goal, which was bringing you to the hotel. Trust Roberta to do what a mother should have."

"Well, the important part is that you're here," Riley replied, a bright smile on her face. "But I want to be the one to ask the question: will you make me the happiest bride ever, by agreeing to sing at my wedding?"

It was quite a comedy, all these people surrounding her, studying her expression and waiting for a reply. Jade saw Aaron Bridges from the corner of her eye, ever watchful, a pen in his hand, a black notebook resting on the table. His serious demeanor reminded her of the press, which made her leery of making a commitment. She wanted to run and hide. If only she didn't need the money.

"I find myself in the awkward position of having to say yes, for financial reasons alone. But out of kindness to you, Riley, I must point out the obvious. Having me sing at your wedding could add unwelcome media attention to your special day."

"Because of him? Because of that mouthpiece?" Riley wisecracked, glancing at the reporter. "Not even a raging storm could deter my happiness."

"The groom might," Lilith responded, not looking at her daughter.

Had Jade heard correctly? Riley's face flamed a bright shade of red and Jade just sat there, not knowing what to say. Everyone waited for Riley to respond and she didn't disappoint.

"Mother, cease and desist. We've had this conversation too many times before. Must I remind you that I love Brock? Please, don't make me choose between my mother and my future husband."

Jade took a deep breath, choosing to disregard the hurtful words shared between Mrs. Hamilton and her daughter. "I want to be sure you both understand my circumstances. My past has gained me a lot of bad press and ugly gossip. The alcohol addiction rumors are true, but I'm clean now. I have not had a drink in three months. However, the cravings and the media attention will always be with me, and I don't want my personal life to intrude on your special day. And it could. If I'm at your event, likely the media will be, too."

"The singer has a point," Lilith cautioned, tapping her nails on the table. "This will be a society event and we don't need a drugged-out starlet bringing undue attention to our affairs."

Jade sucked in an astonished breath, her hand flew to her lips. She couldn't believe Riley's mom had been so unkind.

"Mom?" Riley appealed. "How could you be so rude? Jade expresses her honesty and you express your bad manners. You should know better, you're the mayor's wife! Shame on you!"

"I'm pointing out the facts, Riley. You need to consider the bad press and the potential for… drama."

"You have it all wrong. I only need to take into account what I want on my wedding day, and that's not some society event. Mom, I want Jade to sing at my wedding. I don't care about her past. You know what, I'd like to be a part of her future."

The bride suddenly appeared as if she would cry. Jade couldn't bear it, considering her own troubles. "Lilith, Riley, I don't know what has happened to come between the two of you, but love should pull a family together, not apart."

"Pretty smart for a country music star," a woman, separate from the assembled group, tittered. They looked up to see Mrs. Arbuckle. "Do you think you ladies could spare a chair for one more? I don't take up much space."

"Of course, Mrs. A.," Melanie replied, pulling out the empty chair between them.

"Jade Carter, you look stunning today. Wouldn't you say that's true, Lilith?"

"I do confess, I'm jealous of the entire ensemble. Who is your designer, dear?"

"I believe Ralph Lauren."

"Let's get back to the purpose of the meeting," Wendy said, tapping a pen on the table. "I have a formal contract for you to sign, should you agree to sing at Riley and Brock's wedding. The bride is prepared to pay you well. The sum of one-thousand dollars."

"Will you do it?" Riley asked hopefully. "Will you sing at my wedding?"

Jade lowered her head, the emotion was overwhelming and she felt like crying tears of gratitude. "How could I ever say no? To learn that a fan still believes in me warms my heart. Riley, I would be honored to sing at your wedding."

The entire table erupted in applause. Even Lilith, so it appeared to Jade that she had won over the mother of the bride, at least for now. "I'd like to make amends to my daughter, at least on this accounting," Lilith replied. "Ms. Carter is right. Love should bring a family together. Thank you, Jade, for reminding me of that."

"Amen," Mrs. A. said. "Now where's the server? It's time to celebrate."

Riley raised her hand. "There's one more request I'd like to make."

"What else could there be?" Lilith asked.

"Jade, I know this is a lot to ask, but could I convince you to write a song for the wedding?"

"It's been a long time," Jade replied, pondering the request. "I don't know if I have any lyrics left inside of me to write."

Melanie, sitting beside her, patted her hand. "How will you know if you never try? Maybe this is your chance to write a song, a new song could help restore your career?"

Just then, Roberta strolled inside the dining room and begged to join them. Jade broke out in laughter. "Of course you may join us. Pull up a chair," she said, chuckling, so happy with these women surrounding her. These ladies were not her family, but all of a sudden she wished they were, even Lilith Hamilton.

"All right," Jade said, smiling. "I'll try. I'll try to write a song. Any idea what you'd like me to sing about?"

Riley seemed to glow with happiness. "Yes, true love. Like the love you've found with Jason."

"The *love* I've found with Jason?"

"Why, yes." Riley giggled. "Anyone watching the two of you could tell your relationship was *love at first sight!*"

"Love at first sight!" Jade retorted, wondering if what Riley said was true. Nah, it couldn't be. "But she knew love at first sight would make an excellent song title." She leaned closer to Riley, so only she and the ladies could hear. "But I don't know if we're actually in love."

"Search your heart, Jade. When I met Brock, I knew he was

the one. It took me awhile to convince him of that, but we're solid now."

"*Love at first sight,*" Jade whispered a second time, considering how the music might sound. "You know, I really like the ring of that."

Riley flashed her hand, revealing a large diamond on her ring finger. "Me too," she said with a smile as bright as the solitaire on her finger. "Write about it! Write me a song for my wedding."

CHAPTER 12

*S*itting inside the Peaks Bar, Jason tried to listen to what his friend and colleague was saying, but his focus strayed to sweet kisses and other pleasant thoughts, not to mention the hockey game playing on the Television screen between Tampa Bay and the New York Islanders. Though he didn't usually drink this early in the day, he took a sip of amber ale, not sure what Ben had just said, reasoning it was okay to live life to the fullest and enjoy a Big Rock Traditional, regardless of the time of day. He contemplated Jade and the night before, while the cold brew slid down his throat.

"Where's your head at Jason? You haven't heard a word I've said."

He chuckled, remembering. "I knew you were talking; I heard every word."

"Don't give me that. You were not listening. Your attention was somewhere else. You have a dreamy look in your eyes, and I don't think I've seen you so preoccupied before. Could it be you're more focused on your new house guest than your manager?"

Jason took another sip. "Could be. However, I'm not disclosing anything."

"Hot damn, you've just met the girl. How'd she crawl under your skin so fast?"

"Nope, not there."

"Jason, if I didn't know you better, I'd say you were afflicted by a girl's temptation. What did you tell me a few months ago when I first met Melanie? Let me see if I can remember. Let my memory take me back to the day when you said to me: '*You've got it bad for this woman.*'"

"Dig all you want, Ben. I'm not sharing my secrets."

"We could return to the topic we came here for, how to raise funds for the Red Cross to help the efforts in Fort Mac, and how to increase sales in the bar, but with Jade singing even one night a week, we've already increased profits by a hundred percent. Do you think she'd consider singing at a fundraiser? Do you think she'll be staying in Harmony after your pretense of a relationship ends?"

"We'll have to ask the artist about the singing part, but who said anything about breaking up?" Jason grinned, remembering her caresses. "I'm more interested in seeing where our relationship might go, and that my friend, needs time to play out."

"Seriously, you've been a friend for a long time. Is there a real relationship brewing?"

"You know what? I can honestly tell you I don't know. But when life kicks you in the gut and pain squeezes your chest, you have a heart attack and think you're going to die, once you're breathing again, a man hungers for every possibility that life has to offer. So, I'm game to explore our feelings for each other. In fact, I want to explore whatever is happening here."

calendar. "Say, Saturday, May 21st? Gives Melanie time to do some advertising and Wendy time to take care of the event planning. I realize it's short notice."

"It's enough time," Jade replied, squirming on her seat. "I'll be there. I'd like to support the community."

"All right," Ben acknowledged. "This is going to be great."

CHAPTER 13

Standing near the Thomas Lounge, Jade kissed Jason goodbye. She nestled close to his chest and entwined her fingers within his, loving the way her heart pitter-pattered simply from standing near him. She didn't want him to leave.

"What will you do while I'm at work?"

"My Rover is parked in the lot. If it's all right with you, I'll return to the cabin. That reporter is still hanging around the hotel and he makes me uncomfortable."

"I'd box the man's ears if I could," Jason said with a frown, breaking their contact to retrieve something from his pocket. "But it's probably better to give you this instead. You'll need it."

Jade contemplated the silver key held between his thumb and forefinger. "Jason Knight, are you entrusting me with the key to your castle?"

"If you promise to take good care of it. And you know what," he suggested with a grin, "my home could use a thorough dusting and I don't think we made the bed this morning…"

Jade shook her head, disregarding his suggestive comment. "I'm not much of a maid. I'm sure Poppy has told you."

"You could learn. I could teach you." He grasped her hand, placed the key inside her palm, then squeezed her hand shut tight. "Don't lose it, darling."

Jade studied the key, feeling its weight while considering a man's faith in her, a man who didn't know the real Jade Carter. A few weeks ago, her life had been turned upside down and she'd had to return her key to the Agency. Holding this piece of insignificant metal meant everything.

"Seriously, Jason," Jade mumbled, "are you sure?"

"Hey, don't sound so serious. It's okay; I trust you," he said softly, pulling her back into his embrace. "What, you're going to steal my coffee grounds? I don't think so. Look, I know what I'm doing here, unless there's a reason you're afraid to take the key?"

"My issues don't include theft. What more could there be to talk about?"

"No more talk, just a kiss to say goodnight and to give me something to remember in the coming hours."

Jade smiled, then rising on the balls of her feet, kissed his lips. "Maybe later, if you're not too tired, we can…"

"I'll hold you to your promises, sweet vixen, but I need to get to work. Ben doesn't appreciate tardiness in his employees."

"Don't let me keep you from the customers. In fact, I see Mrs. A. is coming this way. She'll expect her nightly medicinal."

"Okay, darling." He kissed her quickly on the lips. "Off with you then, but if you need anything, anything at all, call my cell."

"I'll do that," Jade replied with a smirk. "If you give me your number."

"What? I haven't given you my cell number?"

"Nope!"

Jade pulled her phone from her pocket and entered the

information that Jason gave her, said a final goodbye and then left his company.

She was preparing to leave the hotel when she saw Poppy. Even from a distance it was clear that her new friend was upset. She waved at Poppy, urging her to come closer.

"What's wrong?" Jade asked, jingling her car keys in her hand.

Jade noticed that Poppy's cheeks were flushed, her blonde hair was styled in messy disarray, and her breathing seemed anxious. She ran her hand through her blonde hair in obvious exasperation.

"I can't do this anymore," she complained. "Tessa called in sick and with her absence, there's no one cleaning the lower floors. The new girl is not working out." She raised her hands in frustration. "Does Ben think I can clean this entire hotel by myself? If it wasn't for my VISA requirements, I'd quit."

"Is it true?" Jade asked. "There's no one else on the schedule, except you?"

"Well, not exactly. Vera's managing the upper floors and training the new staff, but other than that, no one! I keep telling Ben he needs to hire more help."

"I'm sure management is aware of the problem and advertising for more employees," Jade appealed, "but I tell you what. How about you and I grab a coffee and then I'll help you."

Poppy observed the space around them, and then bridging the gap for privacy, lowered her voice. "But Mr. Thurston told me you're no longer able to help me."

Jade grasped Poppy's elbow and led her toward the Alberta Rose Coffee Shop. "Ben told me on my first day at the hotel that I needed to earn my stay. Nothing has changed. Furthermore, I make my own decisions. Poppy, I'm capable of playing the maid.

You of all people should know, since you taught me my skills. And, more importantly, I don't mind. I want to help."

"But look at you." She openly stared, almost gawking at Jade's expensive clothing. "You're not dressed for cleaning hotel rooms. You'll ruin your designer clothing."

"If you're so worried about it," Jade beckoned, amusement lighting her eyes, "get me one of those dreadful cotton uniforms, and then my clothing won't suffer."

"Okay," Poppy simpered, her smile returning, her attitude brightening. "I'll make it up to you. After work, I'll buy you a drink at The Wobbly Dog."

Rule number two, Jade considered. *Don't entertain an addictive situation.* She dared not go to such an establishment as The Wobbly Dog.

"That's okay. I really couldn't. I promised Jason I'd return to his cabin."

"But, he's working tonight, isn't he?"

"Yes, he is."

"So, you'd be going home to an empty house?"

"It's not about that," Jade affirmed, not wanting to admit her weaknesses or addictive tendencies where prying ears could overhear their conversation.

"Then what?"

"Don't pry. Let's get our coffee and then clean the rooms. Poppy, time is wasting."

THE HOURS PASSED QUICKLY. Jade and Poppy scoured bathrooms, made beds, or vacuumed up the carpet crumbs from messier guests. Soon enough, the guest rooms were restored to pristine condition and polished with the fresh scent of lemon. Jade had never toiled so hard in her life, but surprisingly, the effort had inspired an inner joy. Side by side, they had cleaned in perfect harmony, with each sharing their life stories, such as childhood escapades and the crazy exploits they had carried out as young girls.

Poppy's baby blue eyes had shone with happiness while sharing her stories of surfing the ocean waves of Bondi Beach, camping on the shores of Jervis Bay, or drinking beer until the wee hours of the morning with her many friends. Her life seemed idyllic and cozy. The girl's spirit teemed with excitement and adventure. Who wouldn't want to climb on a surf board and be her friend?

Jealous, Jade frowned. In comparison, her formidable years had been dreary. She hadn't had the luxury of many friends. She reflected on hot summer days running through the water spray of a sprinkler with a cousin, or swimming at the local pool, often alone. She didn't want to admit it, but her friends had been few.

"Gosh, I love the ocean. Maybe someday I could travel to Sydney, to those beaches you've told me about, and you could teach me how to surf?"

Poppy beamed with excitement. "I'd love for you to come over, but…"

"But what?" Jade asked, gesturing with the duster. "You think I couldn't handle it?"

"Well, it's a long flight and more to the point, you're all phish posh and stuff."

"I'll have you know, Poppy Ellis, when I was younger, I could ride my bike up and down almost any hill. I was a real daredevil. I did jumps."

Poppy shook her head. "You didn't," she said, laughing, "you're lying."

"For real, I did! I may have changed with fame and fortune, but I can still wear a one-piece bathing suit like any other girl, and I'm not afraid to wade into the water."

"If you say so, itsy-bitsy, yellow polka-dot bikini." Poppy giggled, and together, they left the final room. "But can you take a leap into the ocean? The water's cold and you could be bitten by a shark straightaway."

Jade considered the image that came unbidden to her mind. She'd encountered many fish with teeth equally sharp during her career. They were not animals but they might as well have been. "I can't imagine that every swimmer is attacked."

"Of course not," Poppy reasoned, reaching for the cleaning cart, soon pushing it along the hallway. "But there's always the chance. Can you swim?"

Jade followed behind Poppy, contemplating. "I'm not a strong swimmer, but yes, I can swim. Although I've never ventured too far into the ocean."

"Then before you come over, you should take lessons to strengthen your swimming ability. And then, country music star, I'll take you into the ocean for the ride of your life! I'll teach you to surf."

The work didn't end with cleaning guest rooms. Poppy and Jade continued their conversation in the basement of the hotel while washing hotel laundry. By the time the sheets and towels were washed and folded, it was nearing 10:00 p.m.

Jade had enjoyed Poppy's companionship so much, she didn't want to say goodbye. She almost felt sad changing back into her checkered shirt and navy pencil skirt. Tired, they climbed the stairs together, laughing as they entered the hotel's lobby.

"Jade, I'm not ready to leave your company. We've had so much fun together and I really appreciate that when I needed support, you helped me. Please, join me at The Wobbly Dog for a drink. I'll buy."

Jade bit her lip, dangling her keys in her hand. The idea of accompanying Poppy to the pub lit her taste buds on fire. She didn't want to go, but could visualize holding a glass of vodka in her hand. She searched for an appropriate excuse and came up empty. "I really shouldn't go. It's getting late."

"Come on, Jade. Don't be a stick in the mud. What could one drink hurt?"

"You have no idea," Jade mumbled, worrying about her weakness.

"Is it the alcohol?" Poppy asked. "You know, I won't force it down your throat. You can drink whatever you want, no one will judge you for having a glass of coke."

Jade placed her car keys in her pocket, sweating, licking her lips. She didn't know where the sudden craving to imbibe came from. She didn't feel well. Anxiety caused her head to ache, her throat to constrict, and her tastebuds to heat with cruel need. She wanted a drink desperately, but she was too ashamed to admit this to Poppy. She was in terrible trouble and she knew she should be contacting a counselor for help.

"How far is it?"

"Not far. We can walk to the pub from the hotel."

"Okay," Jade agreed, hoping for inner strength. "I'll come. But one drink and one drink only." *One drink* wouldn't hurt her.

"You have as many as you want," Poppy purred, motioning

toward the main doors of the hotel. "I'm having at least two. It's been a long day. I can already taste the amber."

"Me, too," Jade said with a grimace, knowing she shouldn't be entertaining these emotions. She swallowed, following Poppy from the hotel. They walked along Main Street, passing several quaint buildings, every step taking them closer to temptation and the beverages waiting inside The Wobbly Dog pub. The closer she came to the pub, the stronger the thirst and cravings grew.

Jade was soon sitting on a bar stool inside the establishment, peering at the bartender, Cliff, and all the pretty bottles lined up behind him. *Temptation.* She licked her lips.

When the bartender placed a beer in front of Poppy, and a Perrier with a jigger of real lime juice in front of her, Jade stared at Poppy sipping her drink, unable to look away from the amber beer, or even focus on their conversation.

A handsome young man sat beside Poppy, and she struck up a conversation with him.

"G'Day, mate." Poppy blushed, giggling as she began a private tête-à-tête, soon ignoring her friend. Jade imagined what that drink would taste like as it passed over Poppy's lips.

"Damn it!" she muttered, sipping her non-alcoholic beverage. It just didn't satisfy her craving. *Just one.*

"Bartender," Jade called out, sliding the glass away. "Give me what my friend is having."

"Atta girl!" Poppy whistled, nudging Jade with her arm, toasting in her direction when the bartender placed her drink on the bar top. "Cheers!" She saluted, clinking her glass.

Everything after the first drink was soon a blur.

~

MUCH LATER, the music in The Wobbly Dog pub grew to a rocking crescendo as a dancer took to the stage. Jade's stomach roiled with illness and her head ached with pain. She didn't know how many shots the bartender had slammed in front of her; she simply couldn't remember. Maybe she'd had one too many, or maybe someone had dropped an illicit drug in her drink. She realized it was time to return to the hotel. She had to leave; she'd made a big mistake and she felt sick.

She slowly rose from the bar stool, her head spinning with dizziness as bright stage lights captured the metallic surface of a mirror ball, *turning*, blinding her eyesight.

I need to leave—she thought, staggering to the exit.

Grasping the brass handle, Jade pulled the door open and stumbled into the cool night, leaving the pub. She shuffled along the sidewalk of Main Street, *swaying*, stumbling. She was only slightly aware of her head buzzing as if a cold had invaded her sinuses, blinding her ability to think rationally or reasonably as she made her way.

A camera's flash of light confounded her. She unconsciously considered the white explosion, glancing toward the illumination, then lifted her hand to her aching head, trying to return to the hotel, clutching her stomach. Sick. She was going to be sick.

A second flash—

Diamonds stabbed at her eyesight. She wobbled and fell to her knees, scraping them against the concrete sidewalk, but not sensing the pain. She lounged there for a moment, *dizzy*, sweating, only slightly aware that her nylons were torn and that blood and dirt soiled her knees.

"Let me help you—" a voice seemed to call from the abyss.

Jade gazed upward, seeing an elderly man wearing a navy

blue sports jacket. He reached toward her and she tried to grasp his wrinkled old hand, but she fell to the sidewalk. When he reached for her again, she wondered if she was experiencing some sort of hallucination. She just couldn't grasp his hand!

But then she heard his voice. How was it possible? "Rise from the ground, missy. You can do this. Your life depends on it."

Why was he yelling?

"Okay…" Jade blubbered, sensing the stench of alcohol wafting rotten from her breath. Rising to her knees, she retched, losing her stomach contents.

"It's all right, I have you." An embrace grazed against her back and then a camera flash blinded her again. She didn't understand what the continued light meant, unable to make the connection, but somehow she climbed to her feet, unaware of where she was walking along the sidewalk. But someone or something propelled her along Main Street until she grasped the brass handle on the front door of The Thurston Hotel.

Jade wobbled across the lobby, not really seeing the front desk clerk whose hands shot to her mouth in surprise. It was late. Jason might not even be here. Maybe a hallucination stood in front of her now. A crazy image blurred from drinking. Another apparition, he wasn't real.

"Jade?" he spoke, his forehead furrowing with concern, and then anger. "Where have you been?"

When Jade heard her name, she turned toward the sound, seeing Jason standing near the reception desk, hands on his hips. *Why was he angry?*

"Jason?" she mumbled, collapsing to her knees.

She gazed upward, taking in his concerned expression as he

came to her, pulling her upward, a dead weight in his arms. She relaxed like a rag doll, collapsing against him. *Flash!*

"Get out of here," Jason yelled at the photographer and then appealed to the night desk clerk. "Angelina, call Ben."

Jade heard his urgency, but she was too far-gone to do anything but sleep. She slumped against his chest. The fatigue drew her someplace deep within herself. She closed her eyes. She heard someone *calling* her name, *patting* her cheeks, *begging* her to wake up. Her eyelids fluttered open for a second, but overcome with fatigue and substance abuse, they drooped shut again. Despite his efforts, she drifted further away.

He clutched her closer.

"Angelina, call an ambulance!" Jason shouted. "Jade needs help. She needs help now!"

Jade tried to talk, tried to tell Jason not to worry, as she'd been through this before, but a painful buzzing intoned between her ears and she couldn't form the words, let alone use her voice. She slipped further away, *sinking* into oblivion, to rest, to peace.

"Taylor," she whimpered, "help me…"

CHAPTER 14

Several days had passed since the alcohol poisoning. After a horrendous week of watching Jade suffer, Jason pondered her calmer expression, alert to her easy breathing. She slept peacefully now while he reflected on his own fatigue. A walking dead man, he was weary to the bone and exhausted from the constant strain and unimaginable hell each of them had suffered.

The worst of the experience and subsequent withdrawal angst was over. He was grateful Jade slept peacefully, snuggled in the blankets on the bed, yet he reflected on the past week when he'd been forced to watch her uglier personality, her body twisting, writhing in agony, begging him for an alcoholic beverage. Having no addictions of his own, he didn't understand her struggle. He had watched her facial expressions change from apparent beauty to an ugly not so nice demeanor. Needing a break from the battle, he was grateful when she was able to rest, for when she awoke the bad behavior could begin again.

He had been forced to suffer through periods of gentle

persuasion: "Please, Jason," she had begged, "I need a drink. Get me a drink."

To invoked anger: "Damn you! You're a bartender. You know how to shake a martini, so do your duty and bring me a 'colorful language' drink!"

He saw that the real Jade Carter, the woman he had first met, was slowly returning to her kinder and more balanced self. Only now, he understood what climbing into bed with a country star had cost him, and he didn't know if he wanted to pursue this relationship any further. The risk was there for Jade to use again.

Still, he couldn't leave her. He wouldn't leave her. He didn't even know how to contact her family.

"Jason," she appealed, finally awake, "you're tired. Go home."

He inhaled deeply, stood up and began pacing in front of the hospital bed. He paused to scrutinize her directly. A part of him wanted to do as she requested. "Believe me, I want to go home."

Showing no emotion, Jade appeared calmer. The woman he had first succumbed to was still attractive, even though no makeup highlighted her features. Her pale skin showed signs of her recent exploits; gray shadows stole the light from her hazel eyes and her cheeks were blotchy pink from lingering tears. However, he still saw her worthiness and her beauty, not even the pale blue hospital gown could conceal her good looks.

"I can see how hard this has been on you. Why don't you leave? What keeps you here?"

He stood in front of her bed staring at her, calmer now, his emotions under control. Yet he wondered when the next shoe might fall. "I honestly don't know. I guess something important is keeping me here."

"How long have I lain in this bed?" she whispered, stretching, arching her back. "And have you been with me the entire time?"

"You've been in this hospital a week. Dr. Sheridan thought it best for your recovery. I've been with you almost the entire time."

She nodded, appearing so much like a child in that moment that Jason almost stepped toward her. But she wasn't a child. She was an adult woman and he wouldn't enable her to continue this behavior. She had to take some responsibility for her choices if she wanted to get well.

"Did I embarrass myself?"

"Are you asking if your actions are fodder for other people's imaginations? Laid out well for the daily news? The answer is yes. Your drunken images have been published everywhere. The only good news to come from your relapse is that the media are now camped in front of Harmony Hospital instead of The Thurston Hotel."

"I'm sorry, Jason."

"I'm sure you've made your apologies before, maybe to someone other than me," he replied, trying to feel emotion or sympathy that would help him forgive, but he could still feel her nails raking along the side of his face for spurning her repeated requests. An act much different from the sweet vixen he had experienced in his bed.

"Where did you get those scratches?" She asked suddenly.

He turned away from her, choosing to ponder the hospital window and what lay beyond, not wanting to admit the truth. Not wanting to hurt her.

"Did I do that to you?"

He turned back. He wouldn't keep the truth from her and

she must face her ugliness in order to account for her bad behavior. "Yes, Jade. You hurt me."

"I don't know what to say." She shook her head, sighing. "I'm sorry."

Jason watched the tears collect in her eyes. He considered the emotion crumpling her cheeks and quivering her lips. He stepped toward her, remembering his own fight for life. Could he help Jade Carter in her struggle to gain back her life, too?

"I think it's time to discuss your addiction. It's obvious to me that I must understand the complications of addiction, if we're to continue our relationship."

"How could you entertain anything but leaving, after this?" She stared at him with surprise, raising her hands in appeal. "It's wrong to bring someone into my life and make them face my issues, my demons. I can see that I've already caused enough grief in your life."

"I want to support you," Jason huffed, drawing his hand through his hair. "Hell if I know why. I don't believe in love at first sight, but even after seeing you at your worst, I still want you."

"What if I scratch you again? I could, you know."

"Dr. Sheridan says that with the right support and treatment, you can learn to overcome your addiction."

"I thought I was recovering," Jade murmured, nibbling her lip. "I've been trying and that's the honest truth."

Jason made the decision right then and there. He stepped forward and sat beside her on the bed, reaching for her, taking her hand in his. To have and to hold, he considered. "Jade, I want to help you through this, but you have to want to help yourself, too."

"What do you need to hear from me, Jason? What do you want me to say to you?"

"The truth, Jade. I want you to share the good, the bad and the ugly. The alcohol, the drugs, even what led you to trust in these demons in the first place."

She nodded, she lowered her head in defeat; he saw how she struggled.

"Jason," she stated, pausing. "My name is Jade Carter and I am an alcoholic. I have an issue with substance abuse, but I assure you, I have tried to overcome this dependence. Prior to coming to Harmony, I spent three months at a recovery center. I thought I was on the path to a more peaceful place. I thought…"

"You came close to entering that peaceful place you're talking about." Jason sighed, lowering his head. "I thought you were going to die."

"I don't want to lose my life." Jade gasped. "I don't know what more I can say than that."

"I know." Jason gazed at her, seeing her worry. "What a loss it would have been. Not only for me, but also for your fans. Lost songs, songs never to be sung, written, or heard by anyone."

"Do you think anyone wants to hear me sing, after this mess?"

He squeezed her hand. "I know Mrs. Arbuckle would be heartbroken without your singing voice, Riley Hamilton, too. Don't forget she's a loyal fan. Look, I'm not the only human being who cares about you. The entire Thurston Hotel family, staff and owners, are prepared to stand by you."

The tears started afresh. "Really, Jason? Maybe you're only telling me this because you feel sorry for me."

"I would never lie to you."

"I have so much to atone for, but it comforts me that you would support me. Even for show."

"Honey, this is not a show anymore. This is your future—my future—our future we're talking about."

She rose upward in the bed. "Our future?"

Jason sighed, then pulled her into his embrace, clutching her arms. He saw the fear in her hazel eyes, her face contorted with worry lines. "Our future," he responded with a serious tone, one hand still in her grasp, his other wending its way through thick red strands, pulling her closer toward his lips.

"Are you sure, knowing what you know now?"

He kissed her lips. "I'm sure. I'm ready to take you home, to our home. But there's one more matter we need to address before we leave."

"What's that?"

"I need to tell the media something about your situation. What would you have me say?"

Jade squeezed his hand. "I'm tired of running from the press. Tell them the truth. Tell them what I told you."

"And when they ask about our relationship?"

"Are you certain we still have one?"

"If you're willing to work for it. And if you're prepared to assume every approach and every measure that it takes to get well."

"I'm prepared."

"Then I will share with the media that we're a couple, and you have my full support in your recovery. But there's one more piece of information I need to know before I let you rest."

"What is that?" Jade asked.

"Tell me about your relationship with Taylor."

CHAPTER 15

aylor? Lying in her hospital bed, Jade was seized with fear the moment Jason uttered her former boyfriend's name. She retreated from his embrace, reclined to the pillow and glanced away from his scrutinizing expression. Releasing his hand, she slid her fingers through her hair while studying the window. Frustration consumed her and she didn't know how to respond. Didn't know if she was ready to share her grief-filled story.

"I have to know, Jade. You have to talk about him."

"I want to, but I don't know if I'm ready."

"Look," Jason stated, leaning closer, "if we're going to progress beyond this place, we have to learn to trust each other. I can't support you if you're not willing to talk about this other guy, Taylor."

Jade turned back to Jason, her eyes filling with tears. "He was my everything."

"Your boyfriend?"

"Yes," she whispered, her lip quivering. But she struggled for control, taking a deep breath. "We met early in my career. For all intents and purposes, we were Jade the singer and Taylor the songwriter. We collaborated on many of my early songs. He…"

"Let me finish for you," Jason said, taking her hand back. "He introduced you to your addictions."

"Yes. A little Adderall to keep us awake at night, so we could work late into the morning hours writing music, smoking cigarettes, or having…"

"Sex." Jason finished for her.

She stared at him, realizing he was judging her. "I didn't think there was anything wrong with the behavior at the time. I wrote some of my best songs during that period of my life. But then I became dependent on the drugs and I couldn't stop the horrid wheel from turning."

"When did you write *Let me down easy?*"

"When I suspected he was cheating on me, moving away from what we had built for a better prize. He told me my habitual need grew from my own carelessness because I couldn't handle the drugs, or the alcohol. Told me I was a first class loser."

"Sounds like the man was a real class act."

"I loved him." Jade inhaled deeply, almost moaning. "Even so."

"I'll never understand why women put up with that type of abuse and then call it love. Put the man in the past where he belongs," Jason quipped, squeezing her hand, "you want a lasting love, something stronger than the lyrics of a song."

Jade contemplated Jason with some seriousness. At that moment, not wanting a drug, or even a cigarette between her fingers, not even a drink of booze. She hungered only for him. "I do want a lasting relationship. Isn't that what every man and woman hopes for?"

"I think so."

"Why do you want me?"

He surprised her by stroking her face. "Perhaps it's your bright red hair."

"Any girl with a package of dye could mix the same color."

"But I have a preference for gingers as it happens; I can see that underneath your dye job, a true ginger is shining through. That's the girl I'm searching for right now."

Jade giggled, resting her fingers on her mouth.

"What's so funny?" Jason grinned.

"Well—" she started to sing. "Sit right down and I'll tell you a tale, a tale of a fateful ship."

"Gilligan's Island?" Jason mused, appearing perplexed.

"The Skipper, too." Jade smiled, rising upward on the bed.

"Don't tell me your nickname is Ginger?"

"My father always called me his wee little ginger girl." Her smile slipped away. "I miss him."

"Passed on?" Jason asked.

"Yes." Jade reminisced. "Years ago, but my mother is still alive. I don't see her very often."

"Perhaps we should bring her to Harmony for a visit."

"She wouldn't come." Jade saddened, glancing downward. "I've been such an embarrassment to her."

"It's time to change that. Embrace the future. The future is now."

"What would I say to her if she did come to see me; where would I begin?"

"At the beginning, by acknowledging the truth. We're building a new life. A relationship you can share. Perhaps it will help you write a new song."

"But I haven't done that, not since Taylor."

"Well…" Jason grinned, pulling her back into his arms. "Perhaps the first step of your recovery is writing a new song. And didn't Riley request a song for her wedding?"

"Yes, she did. I'm still uncertain if I can achieve it."

"But, you'll try?"

"Yes, I will. Lyrics and music," Jade said, taking a deep breath. "Jason, right now, I'm really grateful for one letter sent to me by a hotel's front desk clerk. That one piece of hotel stationery has given me new hope."

"Hey, what about me?"

"You, too!" she responded, staring at his eyes, nudging his arm. "I think I love you, Jason Knight."

"Is it true love, Jade? The type of love that Patsy Cline would sing about?"

"Don't tease me, Jason," she exclaimed with a half-smile. "I'm trying to be serious here. But yes, I hope so."

Dr. Sheridan interrupted them when he walked inside the room. "I see our patient is recovering, and returning to good health. I have news for you. We're ready to sign your release papers."

"That's fantastic news," Jade replied, keeping an eye on Jason.

"But before I release our star back into the world, there's a few guidelines I want to share."

"I'm ready, Dr. Sheridan. I can face whatever you have to say."

"I've talked to Jason at length about this already, but with the right support, it's safe for you to leave the hospital. And if you're willing, I'd like to enroll you in our outpatient program, so you can continue to receive the support you need to stay well. Are you all right with entering a treatment program?"

"I'm able and willing," Jade asserted, glancing at Jason. "But if I enter the program, what are your expectations of me?"

"You would come to the hospital daily to meet with our psychologist on an outpatient basis. It's an important next step. Too many people leave the hospital after a setback and end up right back where they started, using again. I don't want to see that happen to you. And with the right support, it won't."

"Jade is coming home with me, Doctor. I've cleared out the liquor from my home and the staff at the Thurston will support Jade, too, watching over her when I'm at the hotel working."

"That's great," Doctor Sheridan said, "but Jade doesn't need a babysitter; she needs to take responsibility for her own welfare. Please ensure the support system is not over-reaching in their assistance."

"I'm sure Jade can take care of such situations on her own."

"Hmm," Jade said calmly. "You know, I don't mind. Normally, I would, but anyone who cares enough to support me right now, I'll appreciate their help."

"Will you enter the treatment program?" Dr. Sheridan asked.

"I will," Jade replied.

"Fantastic! Well then, there's nothing left to do but sign the papers and get the two of you out of here. You take good care of this gal, Jason. She's a keeper."

"I think so, too," Jason declared, patting her hand, "but thanks for your vote of confidence."

The nurse returned with the papers and whispered final words of advice. After she left, Jade dressed in jeans and a thick white T-shirt, and then prepared to leave. Jason soon took her hand and escorted her from the room.

"What will we do when we get home?" Jade asked, holding her pink cashmere sweater.

Jason squeezed her fingers and gave her a compelling look.

"Oh my," Jade exclaimed, shaking her head and setting aside her curiosity, she hurried along the hospital hallway, trying to keep up with Jason's stride. "If you're considering romance, do you think such an exercise is permissible for me, for us, so soon after…"

"Doctor's orders," Jason said with a grin. "He wrote the prescription! However, we have to stop someplace before we go back to the cabin."

"Oh, where are you taking me?"

"You'll know soon enough."

CHAPTER 16

When the doors slid wide, Jade passed through the glass panels, her fingers gripping Jason's hand. She tried to dismiss the commotion outside the hospital and glanced at the wall clock above the doors, which indicated the hour was almost noon. She scrutinized a darkening sky swirling with gray clouds, a weather change that forecasted rain later in the day. She took a deep breath, smelling the moisture, dismissing the photographers who waited for her to leave. She breathed deeply, holding her head high and trying to appear calm, even though anxiety caused her head to hurt and her body to tremble. Jason squeezed her fingers as if he sensed her unease, then led her to his truck that was parked near the curb. Together, they passed over the concrete sidewalk at a well-ordered pace.

"How are you, Jade?" A reporter called out.

"She's doing well, thank you," Jason replied, opening the vehicle's passenger door like a true gentleman and assisting her inside. Once seated, Jade turned away from the photog, giving him her back, focusing on the inside of the vehicle. She couldn't help but notice that luggage and various other items were packed inside the truck's box.

Confused, she stared at Jason as he climbed inside the cab. "Jason, why do you have all this stuff in your truck? I thought we were going to your cabin?"

"You and I," he said with a grin, placing the key in the ignition, "are taking an adventure."

"Really? Do I have some say in the matter? You should have asked me first."

"Perhaps," he replied, as the engine roared to life. "But you've been surviving on the edge for too long, and I thought you should experience life with all its possibilities, without drugs or sad memories of Taylor. Those life struggles are problems of the past, and you must leave them behind to embrace your future."

"Jason, I didn't choose to live my life on drugs."

"You didn't? You didn't choose to take that first pill? You must have known it wasn't a good choice."

"I suppose I questioned my initial intentions when I held the orange demon in my hand." Jade reflected on her past, remembering. "Almost anyone would consider their options, but I didn't know how I would react to the drug. Not then."

He frowned as if he didn't believe her. "You know now, and if you want to survive to see the future, you must adopt a positive change." He sighed, obviously frustrated, but she didn't turn away from his stern expression. She wanted to prove she was serious about her future, and that she could face whatever was to come.

"Jade, I want to show you what life can offer when norms like fresh mountain air is the substance you crave. And a lifestyle change will help to improve your situation, when you combine it with a healthier experience."

"All right. I hear you, but this change of plan comes as a surprise. Though I suppose, what could it hurt setting off with you on a little adventure. I can trust you, right? But you need to tell me, where are you taking me?"

He pulled away from the curb, soon maneuvering the vehicle through the parking lot and away from the press. "Into the wild, Jade Carter. We're going camping for a week. Maybe the birdsong will inspire the song you need to write. Maybe the fresh clean air, even the experience, can offer some healing, too."

Jade turned away, scrutinizing the parking lot and the cars. She should be excited, but she was scared to death. "Why are you doing this? This is crazy. You and I have known each other for the space of, what, a few weeks? I don't know if I'm comfortable with this plan."

"Honey, believe me," he quipped, scrutinizing her with a perturbed expression, "I don't know why I'm entertaining this change in my life either. It's not exactly a picnic, but I bought the basket so I figured I might as well fill the box with prospects."

"I'm not a picnic basket. You can't compare me to an object."

"Certainly not, but you are the risk that kissed me and the odds could be in our favor. Are you game with finding out? Do you remember kissing me?"

"Yes," Jade acknowledged, lowering her head. "I kissed you. A woman could never forget kissing you. I don't want to admit it, but it was my first mistake. However much I enjoyed it."

"Don't say that, sweetheart. I'd like to think it was the first good instinct your lovely addicted heart reached for. Let's go with that and seek the other possibilities."

Jade gazed at Jason. She could see the thoughts weaving in his head, and damn the man, she wished she knew what he was planning. For a surety, he was scheming. Men always thought they could change the future by their actions. She knew she shouldn't compare, but she remembered Taylor and his damnable promises. She didn't want to be hurt again.

"I'm not certain what lies in wait for either of us," Jade stated. "Either within your secretive plans, or inside your cabin. I don't know what to do."

"You can start by trusting me." He smiled slimly. "I won't hurt you."

Jade nibbled at her lip. "Taylor said that, too."

"I'm not Taylor. Please don't mention his name again. I need to protect my heart, so I'm careful about what goes inside this body. You need to learn the same life lessons, too."

Jade took a deep breath. "All right. I hear you. Take me into the wild. I'm ready to sing."

He chuckled. "I'm ready to do an entirely different act, but that can wait."

Jade giggled, gazing at him. "Jason, let's take it one day at a time."

"For sure, but a body craves its exercise."

"I imagine the heart does too, and you know that I want a love ever-lasting."

"So you've said," Jason replied, staring straight ahead. "So you've said."

Jade was feeling pretty good as the truck slowly traveled along Jasper Avenue headed south. Not knowing much of the town yet, she didn't think anything untoward was occurring, not until Jason took a left turn and drove into a parking lot. She sucked in a breath when the truck stopped directly in front of The Wobbly Dog pub.

"Jason," she appealed, cringing, her tone sharp. "Why are we here?"

"We're here to face your demons," he said, turning off the ignition. Jade's stomach fell as the engine expired to silence. She clutched the armrest, not wanting to exit the vehicle.

"Jason, my demons are the drink and they're waiting inside the pub."

"I know. You're beginning your recovery by facing them."

She watched him climb out of the truck and firmly close the door. She scrutinized him as he walked around the front of the cab, coming to her side and opening the door. He was dressed in a black down jacket with a turquoise flannel shirt tucked inside his jeans, and she wanted to climb into his arms, but she stared at his amber eyes instead, feeling lost.

"Come on," he urged, "come on out."

Panic suffused her chest. "I can't go in there."

"You can and you will. Honey, I'll be right beside you, all the way."

Jade stepped from the truck and was soon standing on the asphalt. Clean of drugs, *again*, she was shaking. "I really can't go in there."

He pulled her into his arms. It didn't escape Jade's notice that cameras were snapping pictures. She gazed at the lens of the photographer, knowing the fear coiling inside her stomach was fully displayed on her face. The photog grinned. She knew the image would gain him an excellent reward.

"Jason, the cameras are capturing this."

"Let them. This is the new Jade Carter embracing the past and accepting the future. Let your fans see you trying to regain your life, too. Now, forget the rat pack, let's go, back inside the pub."

Still, Jade held back, afraid, even though Jason held out his hand. "You know, darling, I'm going in there with you. You won't face this alone."

"All right!" Jade cried out, placing her hand in his warm grasp, persuaded to follow him inside.

Jason pushed against the thick wooden door and it swung inward. Jade hesitated for a moment, standing on the threshold, but then supported by his strength, she walked through the entryway into what she now considered the devil's holding house. She considered the dance podium at the far end of the establishment. She studied the hanging lights, almost feeling the heat against her skin.

A poster of a provocative woman, *Misty Dawn*, reminded Jade of the many occasions she'd been forced to sing inside such establishments early in her career. She should be comfortable inside this space. She cringed instead, not wanting an unclean life any longer.

Jason nudged her forward, and she soon stood in front of the walnut bar. Surprisingly, Poppy waited there, her expression forlorn, sitting on the exact barstool she had lounged on the week before.

"Take a seat next to Poppy. Just like you did on that night," Jason stated, ushering her forward with his outstretched hand. She permitted him to take the lead.

"I'm so sorry," Poppy cried as she came forward. The tears threatened, pooled in her baby blue eyes, soon escaping to slide down her cheeks. "I didn't know."

"This isn't about you," Jason stated. "We're here to help Jade, and that's all. Ladies, take your seats."

Jade did as Jason requested, sidling up to the bar and sitting on the barstool. Poppy wiped at her tears while Jade focused on the bartender.

"What can I get you folks?"

"I'll have a Traditional beer," Jason replied.

Poppy glanced at Jade, Jason, and then the bartender. "I'll have a Sprite."

"Nope, you won't." Jason asserted. "Jade must face her demons, and her life shouldn't be affected by your actions. She needs to learn to choose wisely. What will you have, Jade?"

"You sure you want to play it this way?" Clint grumbled, his fingers tapping against the bar top.

"I'm the paying customer, so I'm in charge. What do you want, Jade?"

She bit at her lip, not enjoying the firm tone of Jason's voice. She gazed longingly at the pretty bottles lined up on the counter behind the bartender, and it seemed like every one of them had her name on the label. Absolut raspberry, vanilla vodka, and sweet Jose Cuervo tequila. In fact, the brand didn't matter; she thirsted for them all.

"A club soda with a jigger of real lime," she whispered, swallowing.

"Is that what you really want?" Jason asked.

"No!" she growled, almost yelling, her right hand clenching into a fist. "I especially want that black Sambuca. The hunger will never go away. I'll always want these things. But I can't have them."

"Is it terrible reaching for a healthier alternative?"

Jade watched Clint place a beer in front of Jason, and a Strongbow cider in front of a quiet and distant Poppy. Tears were slipping along the contours of her face by the time the drink arrived, but at least she knew this beverage couldn't harm her in the way the others could. She knew she had to accept change.

"It's not terrible," she mumbled, "but the blatant hunger never goes away. Not ever. And the thirst is unbearable sitting inside a place like this."

"Why?" Jason asked, sipping his beer. "You can get a beer anywhere: at the local liquor store, a restaurant, and if you really want to hide your sins away—imbibe at home. Surely you've been to places like this in your career? And you might have to frequent them again should your career continue?"

"I suppose so." Jade took a sip of her non-alcoholic beverage.

"It seems to me then, that this is the second step in your recovery. To accept the past by sitting inside this demon."

"You're crazy, man," Clint stated. "Leave the girl alone."

"Not on your life." Jason studied her meaningfully. "Have you had enough of this hell?"

"I have," Jade stated.

"Are you ready to change your life?"

Jade took a sip of her drink. "I'm ready. I told you that before, but the thirst will always be there."

"Life will be there, too." Jason took a big sip of his beer and then placed his glass on the bar top. "What do you say, girls? Leave this bitch behind us?"

Jade couldn't jump off the seat fast enough. "Yes, sir, what's next, sir?"

"Funny you should ask. I think you could benefit from experiencing the thrills of life and I have just the ride for you. Are you ready, Poppy? I know how you Aussies welcome the thrill of the surf and the wild ride over fresh powder."

Poppy gazed at both of them, obviously terrified. "Are you sure about this, Jason?"

"About life? I've never been more certain about anything. Let's go, ladies. After you," he instructed, escorting both of them from the bar.

"Good luck." Jade heard the bartender call as they left.

Jade wondered what Jason had in mind? *Where was he taking them?* Whatever his end game, she suspected she wouldn't like it.

Jason wondered if choosing the white-water rafting trip was a wise idea after all as he drove his truck through the streets of Harmony, soon traveling east along the Trans-Canada Highway toward the Kananaskis River. The tension inside the cab was tangible. Sensing the upset from the ladies, he turned on the radio when the silence lingered too long with both Poppy and Jade refusing to speak to him.

He could see that Jade was angry. Would she be angrier still when she realized where he was taking her, or would she welcome what he had in mind and accept the challenge? Somehow, he didn't think so.

The silence lingered as he turned onto Highway 40, heading south along the Kananaskis Trail. Finally, he propelled the truck along a side road at the Widowmaker turnoff, slowly meandering to the parking lot.

Jade stared ahead, perhaps considering the various pine trees, but then she turned away from the passenger window, considering him with a curious expression.

"What are you up to, Jason?"

"I suspect you already know. Get ready for a wild ride."

"A wild ride?" she complained, scowling, her mouth open in shock. "You're not taking me on that river!"

He grinned, chuckling. "I most certainly am, sweetheart."

Poppy shook her head. "This is not the way I planned to experience my first rafting trip, but since your boyfriend is set on riding the white-water, I'll try to look forward to it."

"I don't want to do this," Jade said, crossing her arms. "And you can't make me!"

When they came around the final bend in the road, Jason heard Jade gasp when she saw that their friends were waiting. He was grateful the Thurston crew had followed through with their promises. They stood near the outhouse on the fringe of the parking lot, suited up and ready to go. Ben and Melanie Thurston, Bailey, Wendy, and two other people Jade hadn't met yet. He'd introduce her to them soon.

Jason swung the truck into a parking stall, edged the stick into park and then turned off the ignition. If first appearances could describe what the Thurston family might be feeling, Jason saw they were just as unhappy about this rendezvous as Jade. Yet here they were. Dressed and ready, wearing wet suits, wet booties, and PFD devices over top of nylon flash jackets. A bright blue raft waited with the company name, Mountain Jewel, inscribed on the rubber in white lettering. Family, Jason ruminated. He hoped Jade appreciated their efforts on her behalf.

"What the hell, Jason?" she suddenly cried out, her voice wavering. "You're making your friends ride, too? Surely they didn't sign up for this madness? This is not fair to me, or to them. And the weather sucks by the way. It's raining. It's certain to be cold."

Jason turned to Jade, attempting to be firm. "Friends stand by their friends in all types of weather, good and bad. And it's drizzling. It's not a downpour."

She crossed her arms. "I don't like the cold."

Poppy, stuck between the two of them, attempted to bolster Jason's side. "It could be fun?" she ventured, raising her eyebrows as if she wasn't sure.

Jason opened his door. The situation was almost comical. "That's the spirit, Poppy. I knew you would come around."

He climbed out of the truck and held the door open. Poppy slid across the seat and joined him on the asphalt. Jade harrumphed, her arms crossed, not following Poppy's example.

"I want to experience everything Canada has to offer," Poppy began, trying to coax Jade from the vehicle while holding the door ajar. "I've come a long way and I mean to experience it all. Come on, Jade. You can do it. You might even have a good time?"

"All right!" Jade grumbled, opening the passenger door and climbing out of the old Ford. She walked toward the group. "Hi," she called out, already shivering from the cold. "Fancy seeing you in a place like this. The Thurston Hotel is surely missing her management team? Maybe we should forget this craziness so you can all get back to work?"

"Emily is managing the hotel while we're gone," Ben said, grinning. "We couldn't let Jason go down the river alone."

Jason considered their guide, a clean-cut gentleman who approached Jade and held out his hand to her. He owed him for agreeing to chaperone this adventure.

"Now that everyone's here, let's get this party started. I'm Teague Farraday, Miss Carter," he offered, taking her hand in a firm grip. "The owner of Mountain Jewel Sports. I'll be your guide on the river today."

A woman with shoulder length auburn hair held out her hand. "I'm Chastity Howell, famously known as Tea. Buttercup, I don't know how or why I've been roped into this journey, but here I am."

"You know why." Jason coughed into his hand. "Tell the country singer."

"My reputation precedes me," Tea grumbled. "Here we go, Jade Carter. My name is Chastity Howell and I am an alcoholic. Now that the confession is over, Jason thinks I'd make an excellent support for you, both on and off the raft. And in truth, I know the struggles you've encountered, and understand what you've been through too, because I've faced this demon myself. I want to help."

"That's kind of you to offer your support, but it's not necessary. I can manage this temptation on my own."

Tea grasped Jade's arm beneath the elbow. "I know you think you can. But addiction is better shared with friends, friends who understand the struggle. You know, for moral support and stuff?"

"You can share all you want after we've battled the river," Teague declared, taking command. "These three need to get their gear on. I don't think there are any camera's to encroach on your privacy, but for modesty's sake, there's the pit/vault outhouse. It's not ideal. It is what it is."

Jason heard Jade sigh. He could tell she wasn't convinced. About the change room or the upcoming journey.

"So you people are going to make me do this?"

"Not us," Bailey growled, stabbing her finger in Jason's

direction, "Him. Jason!" Her angry voice and annoyed countenance amused him.

"Why?" Jade begged.

"He's holding our secrets," Wendy responded. "It seems you can't say anything to a bartender, regardless if you're a friend or family."

"Spoken like the true sister I never had." Jason chuckled, grinning, his voice succumbing to laughter. "All right then. Let's get our gear on and get ready to go. It's time to launch the boat."

SHAKING SLIGHTLY, Jade sat on the edge of the rubber raft, her right foot tucked under the cross tube, her other foot flat on the floor. One hand white-knuckled the T-grip of the paddle, the other the middle portion of the shaft. Consumed by anxiety, she couldn't remember the safety drill, or any of the other commands as they paddled down the river.

"Paddle!" Teague called out. Jade gazed across the raft, scrutinizing Jason momentarily before she drove the plastic blade into the water. She hoped he saw the anger in her expression and the determination in her stroke.

"Keep at it," Teague yelled as the raft carried them swiftly through the water. "Stroke. Stroke. Stroke."

Whoosh! Jade felt her tummy drop as raft and riders came between two impressive shelves of rock. Water splashed in her eyes as they plunged into the rapids below, descending over a watery break, riding the current like a roller coaster without wheels.

Jason grinned at her, holding his paddle on his lap as the raft sailed along. "See—" he yelled over the strident swish of water.

"It's not so bad. You've just crossed the Widowmaker. You did it, Jade."

She matched his stance, a slight smile shaping her lips. "Hurrah," she blurted out, "I did it," tutting her disapproval while realizing her lips were probably turning blue. "Maybe this isn't so bad?"

Sure, she had vocalized what her lover had hoped she'd say, but she didn't believe in the journey. Not really. She hadn't enjoyed the water assaulting her fair skin at all.

"We'll progress to the Hollywood Hole," Teague declared. "A small play hole on your left. Stroke right. Paddle. Paddle. Paddle. Here we go."

"Oh… buttercup!" Tea yelled as they swiftly sped through a rushing current of water. "Over and down we go…"

Jade paddled when she was told to paddle, soon overcoming her fears. During the calmer stretches, she relaxed, taking in the shoreline, studying the trees, amazed by the miraculous view of mountains rising into a gray sky swollen with precipitation. Even though it was cool, the landscape gave her time to pause, to reflect on her past and consider the future. But she didn't welcome the rougher patches where freezing cold water splashed up and nipped at her eyes. Floating along a calmer creek would have been more to her liking.

"Pay attention," Jason suddenly yelled. "Get ready. We're coming to the Point Break."

Jade nodded at him, frowning, paddling.

She saw two swirling pools of water. *Oh no—*

Jade stretched forward, dipping her blade. Tiring, she'd just placed the blade in the water, when the raft bumped over the ledge, splashing a wall of water at her face. She gasped, choking on the spray, struggling to find a breath. Her foot came loose from underneath the cross tube. She wobbled on the side of the raft, losing her balance. Perhaps seeing she was in trouble, Jason reached for her, but she slid off the edge of the raft and tumbled into the water.

Swoosh. Down she went into the miserable gloom.

The cold stung her exposed flesh almost immediately, shocking her as she sank into the freezing river. She lost her paddle. She kicked up for air, taking a quick breath, remembering not to try to stand as the powerful current propelled her downstream.

"Swim!" she heard someone yell as she bounced along in the raging water, trying to float.

A hand reached to her as the raft drifted near, but she couldn't grasp it. She lay on her back, grateful for the warm gear, screaming at herself to remember Teague's directions, trying to keep her head above water.

Then she saw Jason's face, etched with fear. He had moved to her side of the boat and had retrieved her paddle.

"I'm going to throw you a line," Teague yelled, holding a length of rope in his hands. "Catch it."

With the water rushing past, carrying her downstream, the raft ahead, Jade couldn't hear what anyone was saying. But she saw Teague swinging the rope. It landed short, but she tried to reach it anyway.

She failed. "This is your lifeline," she heard Jason scream. "Take hold. Catch the rope."

The third swing, Jade determined to reach the line. When it came her way, she swam toward the rope and grasped it in her hands. Fingers numb, she somehow held the line as the group reeled her in.

Jason and Teague pulled her to the raft and she landed like a wet fish inside.

"Are you okay?" Jason cried, enfolding her in his arms. "Please tell me you're not hurt."

Jade nodded, gasping for air. "I survived," she mumbled, the words rattling from her. "I have survived..."

"Sorry to have to tell you this," Teague offered. "But we have to finish the run. We can't eddy out until we've traveled below the Green Tongue. Are you up to more than surviving?"

"Green Tongue?" Jade gazed at the Thurston crew, still gasping for breath. Every one of them appeared as if they wanted to quit. The fear in their eyes mirrored her own anxiety. She'd be letting them down if she gave in now. Freezing, she took the paddle that Jason offered her and then climbed back onto the cross tube.

"I won't quit," she cried out. "I'll try to get through this without losing my stomach. Where to next, Mr. Farraday?" she asked, her lip quivering and warm tears escaping her eyes. Not feeling the courage she attempted to show.

He shook his head. "So the lady doesn't shake easily. I applaud your spirit." The raft bounced along. "Are you ready to carry on?"

"I'm... I'm ready," Jade replied, wishing she felt the courage he spoke about. "But I'm going to hold on a little tighter. What's next?"

"The Santa Claus," Melanie groaned.

Jade only heard the *claws* part. She was terrified all over again.

"Paddle," Teague yelled. "Are we ready to have some fun?"

"You betcha," Poppy howled.

The Team broke out in laughter. Jade wished she could see this ride through Poppy's eyes. Perhaps, another time.

～

At the end of the run, they paddled through calmer waters to shore. Exhausted, Jade crawled from the boat and collapsed to her knees at the riverbank's edge. She'd never fought so hard in her life. Her arms ached from the effort, her leg muscles, too. She was content to lounge atop the gravel-strewn rocks, the water lapping against her, even though she knew she should climb the bank to shore.

"Help Jade," Ben called out to Jason. "Teague and I will pull the raft to shore."

Jason grasped her arm and urged her upward. "Come on, sweetheart. Let's get you out of here."

Jade clutched his arm for support, her equilibrium unsteady as she rose upward, soon leaning against him. She faced him, considering his worried expression.

"Do you hate me?"

Jade sighed. "A little. It was a rotten game to play on me, Jason. I'm not an adventurer like you."

"Hey," he whispered, his expression becoming serious. "I'm sorry you fell out of the boat. I didn't think that would happen."

"No sorrier than I," she grumbled, as he led her through a brief expanse of bush, along a muddy trail that led to a campsite. "Forcing me to take a voyage through rough waters was mean-spirited. I was just released from the hospital!"

He appeared wounded by the comment. He stopped in the middle of the pathway, and turned her to face him, taking her hands into his warmer palms. "I didn't mean for you to be hurt."

"That's a short-sighted answer. What did you expect would happen out there? I have no experience rafting."

"I don't know, maybe I thought you'd enjoy the thrill. Maybe, I thought you'd gain inner-strength from the experience."

Jade released him and went to sit on a long fat log. "I gained something all right. It was thrilling; I'll give you that. At least until the *Point Break* where I fell from the boat."

She heard Jason sigh. He sat beside her and pulled her against his chest, but she refused to look at him. "Come on, don't be angry. I obviously made a mistake and I'm sorry."

Jade saw that the rest of the crew was standing near them, listening to their conversation. It was obvious that no one wanted to intrude on a quarrel that should have been private.

"Damn stupid thing to do to a woman," Ben stated.

"Interesting discussion." Teague shrugged. "Don't say I didn't warn you, Jason."

"Hey, I said I was sorry."

"Regardless of the secrets Jason has on us," Wendy said with humor, "you give the word, Jade Carter, and we'll throw him in the river. He knows how to swim."

Jade giggled, not only contemplating Jason's worried expression, but also the Thurston family's need to avenge her.

"You're serious?" she retorted, giggling hilariously. "You'd really do it?" She sighed then, taking in their conspiratorial expressions. "I think one of us in that wild water is enough for one day, don't you?"

"How about some hot chocolate?" Melanie suggested. "The boys can build a fire while the girls change out of our wet clothes."

"Change," Jade whispered. "Where would we do that?"

"Aussie style, in the presence of nature," Poppy replied. "Wrapped in a towel."

"It's either that or walk to the outdoor privy," Teague said, pointing in the general direction.

"My truck is parked close by with provisions," Ben offered. "Melanie can walk you there."

"I think I'll try Poppy's way. I don't want to stand on the cold concrete floor."

Bailey sat down beside Jade. "We took the liberty of packing some warmer clothes for you. Some true mountain gear. You'll need them if you're planning on staying in Harmony. The winters are cold here."

"Who said anything about staying?" Jade grumbled.

Jason appeared crestfallen at her comment. His eyes seemed to lose their brilliance and his facial features diminished to an ashy shade of white. "You're not leaving me, are you?"

Jade regarded Jason's eyes, seeing the worry lines furrowing his brow. It had been a long time since anyone had stared at her with that kind of apprehension. In fact, she didn't think that Taylor had ever looked at her that way. As if he might miss her if she left.

She reached out and cupped his cheek. "Jason, despite your attempt to teach me some sort of lesson, I don't think I could leave you. But," she emphasized in a teasing tone, "I could throw you in the river!"

"Let's do it," Tea yelled, jumping up from the log. "What are friends for but to help each other when the chips are down! Let's give Jason a taste of his own medicine."

Jade giggled, leaning against Jason's forehead as a slow smile played on his lips. "I think you're in trouble. The tables may have turned on you."

"As tempting as it is," Ben exclaimed with an amused chuckle. "How about we get down to hot drinks and food." He stepped forward, soon patting Jason's shoulder. "I think there's been enough team building on the river today."

Jason pulled Jade close, soon rubbing her back. The soft pressure was comforting. He gazed directly into her eyes.

"If I promise to be on my best behavior, can I kiss you?"

Jade nuzzled closer to his lips. "I don't know if I should acquiesce so soon."

Regardless that the group was watching, Jason kissed her gently on her lips. And she liked the soft pressure. Liked it very much!

It didn't escape her notice that Ben pulled Melanie into his arms, too, kissing her on the forehead.

"Stop it, you guys," Bailey called out, shaking her head. "Not all of us *here,*" she emphasized, "has someone to love!"

"All right," Jason grinned, rising from the log, "I'll get the picnic basket. It's full of hot dogs and marshmallows for the fire."

"I'll help," Ben replied, rising from the log and moving toward Jason.

"That leaves me to start the fire," Teague stated, moving to the fire pit. "Ladies, you might as well change."

LATER, the crew sat around a roaring fire, drinking hot chocolate, eating hot dogs and roasting marshmallows. Jade listened to the Thurstons' telling stories about their adventures, and Teague sharing accounts of his various rafting trips. Jade held her mug in her hands, grateful for the conversation and camaraderie that surrounded her. Despite the fact that she had fallen in the river, she was grateful for what she had found after the accident. A sense of family she hadn't known in a long time.

The sight made her miss her mother, but she squashed that emotion down.

"Cheers!" She toasted the group, squeezing Jason's fingers. "To the future."

CHAPTER 18

Jason parked his truck in front of the cabin, shifted the stick into park, then switched off the ignition. He sighed, then glanced at her. Jade saw the longing in his eyes.

"Can we start over?"

"We never ended, darling."

"Can I carry you across the threshold, again?"

Jade giggled. "If you want to."

He opened the truck door and stepped out, then turned to face her. Though she wore a red lumberjack shirt and fleece-lined pants, Jade felt like a princess. He reached to her and urged her to come closer. She slid across the bench and left the truck from his side, soon standing before a tall and handsome man. Her man.

He pulled her close, closer still. One hand rested on her waist while the other rested gently on her bottom. "I've never held a woman who could make my breathing quicken so fast. You're a sight. I like you better in your lumberjack outfit than your designer clothing."

She stepped toward him, never losing sight of the earnest expression in his eyes. She slid her fingers through his hair, relishing the warmth of his skin.

"Jason, honestly, I have never felt more comfortable or warm. Can I confess something?"

"Sure, darling, you can tell me anything."

"Right now, I need you like I need a drink. Is it okay if we take this discussion inside?"

He swung her into his arms. "You won't receive complaints from me. I have plans for you. I mean to satisfy every ounce of your desire."

He walked across the gravel driveway, holding her in his arms, then climbed three wooden steps and strode across the porch to the front door.

"Take my keys, sweetheart, open the door."

Jade did as Jason asked. He soon shut the door with his booted foot.

"The couch or the bed?"

"The bed," Jade asserted, kissing his lips. "I'm cold, I need warmth."

"I'll make you warm." He growled like a bear, nipping at her lips. "All over, and in all the right places."

When they reached the bedroom, Jason placed her on the bed. Jade crawled backwards to the headboard, indicating with her index finger that she wanted her knight to follow.

But he wasn't hasty. He grasped her canvas shoes, removing them, tossing them to the floor.

"What about my pants, darling?" she hinted, reaching for his shirt. "You won't get very far if I keep them on."

"I can help you with the removal. Do you want me to?"

"If you promise to help me, forever."

"That can be arranged!" he teased, grasping the waistband of her fleece pants. Sliding her bottom upward, he swiftly removed the fleece. They too found a spot on the floor.

Jade groaned when he returned to her. His hands explored her legs, his fingers skimming her thighs, squeezing her bare bottom. She giggled when he tickled her belly underneath her flannel shirt.

"Your skin is soft, smooth, like expensive silk."

"I imagine it's even softer, higher," she squealed, as his fingers explored her rib cage, soon baring both breasts.

"Oh, Jason," she gasped, grabbing the small of his back, arching her hips upward, pulling his seeking lips to her mouth. "Kiss me…"

"Where?"

"Everywhere…" she begged him. "Please?"

"I'll satisfy your cravings." His breathing heavy, he pulled away to unzip his fly. Groaning when her hand stole inside his pants.

"What do we have here, mister?" she teased, her fingers twirling in a nest of hair, soon touching his shaft.

"Oh darling—" he moaned, taking her nipple inside his mouth. "I think I need you, need you in the best way."

"Take me. I'm here, waiting for you, begging for you. I need you, too."

Jason backed away, pausing in his pursuit. Jade removed her panties and threw them on the floor.

"What's the matter? Why are you looking at me like that?"

He knelt on the bed, staring at her. He shook his head, and a wondrous expression came over his face. "Ma'am, I just can't believe it. I don't think I've ever held anything in my life, material or otherwise, that has meant as much to me. I want you to know, this is not about sex. I really care about you."

Jade lowered her gaze momentarily, not knowing what to say. Finally, she invited him to come closer. "I know you do. I'm not questioning your motives."

He came closer, studying her eyes. So close, she wondered what he was searching for. "I don't ever want to lose you."

"I know what you're thinking. I can't promise that I won't slip up, but one day at a time, I'll work hard to change my life. I've found a relationship worth fighting for."

He clasped her cheek in his hand, and she leaned into his embrace. "I'll fight for it, too," he whispered, kissing her lips. "Forever. I think I—"

"I know. Enough serious talk. Make love to me."

"You got it, darling!"

She closed her eyes and welcomed his touch. Exquisite sensations flushed her cheeks and fluttered inside her belly. Jason's fingers roamed her body, wandering along her side, caressing the edge of her breasts, and loving her in ways she'd never experienced before. He wasn't hasty. He didn't take his pleasure before ensuring she experienced her own. Soon, they lay entwined together, breathing hard, wrapped in love's cocoon; the physical exploits over too soon.

CHAPTER 19

"Are you hungry?" Jason asked, stroking Jades's cheek.

"Ravenous. What did you have in mind? Breakfast, or something else?"

"Dessert!" Jason grinned, rising from beneath the covers and leaving the bed. Wearing a smile and nothing else, he walked to the ensuite, opened the door and fetched his robe. Curious, Jade watched him retreat from the bedroom.

"After our adventure, I can afford the calories," she called after him. "What did you bake for me?"

"I rarely bake or cook," he said, laughing. "I picked up something special for you at Whimsy yesterday," he offered, holding the doorknob.

"The bakery in town that features cupcakes? You didn't! I love cupcakes!" Jade grinned, hurrying to the front of the bed. "Can I help you? Should I put a pot of coffee on?"

"Nope," he replied, a mischievous smirk on his face. "You stay right where you are. I'm going to serve you, my darling."

"Okay. I'll wait, but hurry back. I'm suddenly famished."

Still wearing the red flannel shirt, Jade reclined on the

pillows, running her fingers through her hair, wondering what was taking Jason so long to return. He finally returned to the bedroom carrying two cupcakes, each nestled inside their own blue box.

"Jason, they look amazing."

"They sure do," Jason replied, placing one of the boxes on the side table. "Mandy Brighton, the owner of Whimsy, is an amazing artist. It's Cinco de Mayo month at the shop and these beauties are a feature of the month. Feast your eyes on sweet cinnamon and sugar."

Jade watched Jason holding the box, suddenly aware that he wasn't giving it to her.

"What are you looking at, Jason?"

He bent down on one knee in front of her, and she stared in amazement at the color of the box. "I know I've asked you this before, and in front of a live audience in my quest to gain a commitment from you. But I want my promises to be offered in private, with only the most important woman in my life listening to my speech."

"Jason—" Jade exclaimed, realizing he was holding a tiffany ring box. "I don't know what to say."

He passed the box into her waiting hands. She accepted the turquoise container with a frosted cupcake neatly fitted inside. Nested within the icing was a rectangular message: *Will you marry me?* Complete with a band of gold set with five amazing ruby stones, resting on a butter cream pillow. Jade remembered where the ring had come from. Mrs. A.

"Beautiful gems set in a band of gold," he whispered, looking at her directly. "But with your consent, the circle could represent *a lasting harmony.* A love you've always wanted, and a song we could sing together for a lifetime."

He came before her, kneeling on the bed. "You won't make me go river rafting again?"

"Not unless we're on a slower moving creek. I must confess, that entire experience was too thrilling, even for a guy like me. Challenged my heart to see you in trouble in the water. I don't want to face that kind of pressure, ever again."

Jade giggled. "I'd actually like to try the river again. But in the heat of summer when falling from the raft wouldn't be so cold."

"The water's always cold, spring or summer. Maybe we could float down Harmony Creek. Start off a bit slower?"

"Ask me, Jason."

He reached for her hand, his facial expression soft and serious. "Jade Carter, the woman I have come to love, will you make me the happiest man on earth, by agreeing to marry me?"

Jade sucked in a breath. She clutched Jason's hand and stretched forward to kiss his lips. "Yes, Jason. I will marry you."

"Oh man," he cried out, obviously relieved. "I was afraid you'd say no. You being a famous country music star and everything."

"I know a good man when I see one."

"We'll have to start making some plans. I suppose you'll want me to move to Vancouver so you can pursue your music career."

"No, I'm not leaving Harmony. This community and its people have become very precious to me. I'll vacate my flat in the big city and move my possessions here. If you're okay with that."

"I'm more than happy with that."

"You won't be when you find out how many pairs of shoes I own."

"We'll build an extension to the cabin. We'll make it work."

Jade clutched Jason closer to her heart with only a cupcake held between them. "I can't believe I found you," she whispered. "I love you, too!"

"Some life circumstances are meant to be, my love."

He pulled back. "But what about your music career. How will it continue from Harmony?"

"My music career…" Jade sighed, eyeing Jason with sincerity. "I don't have a music career anymore. It's the sadness I have not shared with you. I was fired from my contract prior to traveling to Harmony. I don't even have a home to return to."

"I'm sorry, love. Is there anything I can do to help?"

"No. My career is over and it's best I accept the past and move on to embrace my future."

"But won't you miss it? Singing to your fans?"

"Jason, music will always be a part of my life. You know what? You continue tending bar at the Thurston, and I'll sing occasionally for Mrs. A. Any Patsy Cline song that she wants to hear."

"Is that enough for you?"

"It has to be, but there's one more task at hand."

"What is that, my love?"

"Will you put the ring on my finger?"

"I thought you'd never ask." Jason chuckled, reaching for the other box.

"Jason Alexander Knight," Jade gasped, gazing at a one-carat diamond solitaire. "Two rings?"

"Well, yes, my dear, one for the engagement, and the other when you walk down the aisle toward me."

"Do I have to wait to eat the cupcake?"

Jason removed the solitaire from its frosted pillow and slid it on Jade's finger, icing and all.

"I'm in shock," she whispered, taking in the sparkling beauty. Then she took the cupcake from his hands and licked the icing. "You're right, it's delicious! This moment, is delicious, too."

He snickered, pressing his advantage. "Not as yummy as you."

"Jason," Jade giggled, kissing his lips, "after the cupcake!"

CHAPTER 20

Jade stood at stage left beside Jason. She held his hand and gathered the courage to perform in front of an audience much larger than the size she would expect at The Thurston Hotel's, Thomas Lounge. She took a deep breath, dispelling the nervous tension that always came over her prior to performing in front of a live audience, then scrutinized the crowd and the stage she would soon walk across.

The platform, erected for the Fort McMurray fundraiser, had been built at the Town Hall, the only venue that could accommodate a large crowd of people, and it appeared as if almost every resident in the town of Harmony had bought a ticket to attend the outdoor event.

Jade smiled, watching Edward and Lilith Hamilton walk onto the stage to introduce her. A fascinating couple, Jade had come to appreciate Lilith and her odd ways. And while the tension between a mother and daughter carried on, they continued to plan a December wedding. Having seen the pair together, in good times and in bad, she missed her own mother.

Edward stepped up to the mic. While the mayor addressed the audience, Jade glanced at Jason.

"I see your concern, Jade. It's written all over your face. But you've got this. I can't wait to hear you sing and the audience wants to hear you too, or they wouldn't be here. You have to know, if not for your participation, we'd have sold fewer tickets. Just look at the size of the crowd!"

Jade turned away from Jason to study the audience. "It does seem like everyone in town has bought a ticket, but you can't attribute the success to me. Harmony is a strong community. These people will always support families in dire situations, especially families who have been forced to leave their homes due to fire."

Jade knew she had suffered her own troubles, but her problematic life was nothing when compared to the tragedy that Fort Mac residents had faced on the evening of May 3rd, many of them had to drive along a highway with flames shooting on either side of the road. Leaving everything behind, not knowing what they'd return to. It had been the largest evacuation in Alberta history.

"For sure, good people. But everyone loves a country star that has a voice like Patsy Cline. Surely you know, honey, your fans still love you, still want to hear you sing!"

Jade smiled, expressing joy at hearing Jason's support, but she wondered, did her fans still care about her? Did they want to hear her sing? She certainly couldn't dismiss the cacophony coming from the crowd.

"Mrs. A. is hoping for one or two of her favorite songs, but I'll have to focus on my own music tonight."

"Break a leg," Jason said, squeezing her fingers.

Edward made the announcement the crowd had been waiting to hear: "Please give a warm welcome to Jade Carter, Harmony's very own country music star."

The crowd erupted in applause. Holding her guitar, Jade sauntered across the stage and stepped up to a silver microphone stand. She smiled, sighting the band that had been waiting for her. She couldn't believe it, seeing her former bandmates here in Harmony. Jason had contacted Dixon Reed regarding the fundraiser and he'd come through in a big way, not only for the town, but also for her by supplying her band. Grateful, she smiled at the boys and they responded to her expression, giving her a thumbs up, then waiting for their cue to start. She nodded her head and mouthed *thank you*. It appeared that her music career was in reach, if she wanted it back. *Did she want it back?*

She wasn't leaving Harmony. Not now, not ever. The town of Harmony *and her friendly people* had changed her life for the better. She'd entered the treatment program and one day at a time, she was reshaping her life. Stronger, her fingers more controlled, she reached for the mic.

"Good evening, how's everyone tonight?"

The crowd cheered, whistled, some fans screamed her name. *Jade Carter, Jade Carter.* My goodness, the sound of her own name made her smile and had an emotional effect, which a month earlier might have made her cry. She breathed deeply, preparing to sing. The excitement stirring in the air filled her heart with joy. She raised her hand for quiet and the crowd responded.

"Thank you," she said, swallowing. "I dedicate this song to the people of Harmony, who have given my life new meaning in the Rocky Mountains of Alberta."

Aaron Bridges, that seemingly nasty reporter, sat in the front row with a pen, paper and camera, scrutinizing every word she said. Jade giggled into the mic, giving him a thumb's up.

"Even you, Mr. Bridges. I've finished writing a new song. I think you'll get the idea when you hear the headlines."

"One, two, three, four…" she counted into the mic. The band began to play and the singer took up the song, swaying to the rhythm.

> Sometimes a girl gets lost in a whirl,
> with no hope springing from the clouds,
> walking through life,
> fighting the strife,
> not knowing where to turn.
> And then comes a man,
> picnic basket in hand,
> to offer up some hope.
> Singing a song,
> white washed and long,
> A Lasting Harmony…
> Together, we will be—

∼

JASON WATCHED his country music star singing.

Jade Carter, a vision of loveliness in her red sparkling dress, and she really did sound like Patsy Cline. She didn't shy away from the mic and her voice carried over the crowd in sweet waves. The crowd started to clap along with the music, swaying back and forth. He watched men and women singing. It was how it should be. A singer and her audience, almost connected. Singing. Dancing. *Harmony.*

It made him happy to see this woman's transformation. Jade was stronger and more confident every day, but he had one more surprise for her and he hoped she'd understand.

CHAPTER 21

With the arrival of the New Year, Jason knew an important conversation couldn't be avoided any longer. He gritted his teeth, keenly aware the time had come to confront New Year's resolutions, relationship goals, and Jade's music career.

He didn't know why he'd kept silent about his communications with the Agency. Perhaps it was better to distract himself from a telling conversation by staring out the window, reflecting on a blanket of freshly fallen snow. Several inches had fallen overnight. He had peered through frozen windowpanes earlier, only to glimpse a winter wonderland on the front lawn. White-tipped pine trees and fat snowflakes falling from the sky was always a beautiful sight, but the volume of snow had posed a difficulty when the highway had been closed. For the time being, they were trapped inside the cabin.

He didn't mind; their situation could be worse. The change in weather might have brought bitterly cold temperatures, but inside the cabin, a couple was warm and comfortable. They sat near each other on the couch, relaxed and seemingly happy with a crackling fire burning inside the hearth. Jade was reading a book to pass the time. It was all a ruse. She entered into a fictional world to avoid real-life issues. Her silence worried him.

He studied her subdued expression where she sat. A sullen silence had cast a shadow on his country star's emotional well being. He knew what the quiet suggested. Nine months had passed since the Agency had released Jade from her contract, and though she hadn't acknowledged the anniversary, Jason surmised the date weighed heavily on her mind.

Singing two evenings a week at The Thurston Hotel didn't seem to be enough. Sure, she enjoyed performing, and she never complained about missing her entertainment lifestyle, but he sensed she missed the appeal of a larger audience. The chanting, singing, and applause from her fans. She swore she loved this country life, the quiet and the serenity, the friendships made, but it was apparent to her future husband that the time had come to take action, if only to help the love of his life face the future.

"Are you happy, Jade?"

"That's a fully loaded question," she replied, laying her book on her lap. "Yes, of course I am. Why do you ask?"

"I'm trying to decide if the time has come for the two of us to travel to Vancouver. Maybe visit your mother; maybe have an overdue talk with Dixon Reed?"

She heaved a sigh, her forehead furrowing. "My mother doesn't want to see me, and what good could come from a meeting with Dixon? Jason, you know my music career is over."

"It doesn't have to be. I think you've been locked up inside this cabin for too long. You're too quiet, and it's not the winter doldrums getting you down. I think you're either missing your old life, or you're bored to death of me."

Jade's facial expression took on a calm yet perplexed look. "You, my love, will never bore me."

"I know you don't want to talk about your past, but we have to. Do you want your music career back? A fool could tell you've been yearning for something more than a bartender and a crowd of Harmony townsfolk."

She tossed the fantasy novel on the couch and rose to a standing position, suddenly clasping her arms. She walked to the fireplace and stood in front of the stone facade, her back to him. "Honestly, I don't know if I miss the music, but I do miss the money. I don't contribute to our finances; I'm completely beholden to you and I don't like it. Makes me feel guilty. I don't want to use you."

"I don't see it that way. You're soon to be my wife. I want to take care of you."

She turned to face him. A slight smile raised her cheeks upward. "I appreciate your consideration and thoughtfulness, but I want to contribute fully to our relationship. You know, be an equal partner. Plus, I need to take care of myself. I have my pride."

"Jade, I hope what I have to say won't upset you."

Her eyebrows rose upward. "What have you done?"

What had he done? How would she react when he told her? He'd best start by telling the truth.

"I contacted Dixon Reed," Jason said, drawing in a breath. "I made an appointment for you to meet with him early next week. I'll understand if this news upsets you, but I…"

"What did you do?"

"You heard me."

She closed her eyes and placed the palm of her hand against her forehead. "I can't believe you've done this. You should have asked me first. My situation has not changed and meeting my former agent won't make a bit of difference."

"You can't know that. You're a stronger woman, a healthier woman. You might not be ready to confront the future, maybe because you're fearful of further rejection, but you owe it to yourself—and your fans—to talk to Dixon. Educate yourself, Jade. After the conversation, you might not want to pursue a new contract anyway."

She opened her eyes, fully alert to what he'd just said. "What about a contract?"

Jason rose from the lounge chair and took Jade's hand into his own, then guided her back to the couch. "Dixon is considering offering you a new contract. I assured him that you're clean. Free of drugs and approaching life in a healthier, happier, and whole new way."

"You spoke to my former agent on my behalf?"

"I laid the facts on the table in a precise way. He was open to the discussion, although he did have a few questions. When it comes to future business arrangements, we can't blame the man for taking a cautious approach."

"Dixon has always been a serious minded individual." Jade's expression paled. She shook her head. "I can't believe you talked to him, Jason. I wish you'd asked me first."

"Let me explain." Jason squeezed her hand. "I wanted to give your career prospects a gentle nudge, hopefully gaining a positive resolution for your career. And honey, I'm a businessman. I'm not afraid to pick up a phone and initiate a conversation. I had the best of intentions."

"You've caught me by surprise. This is a lot for me to consider. I need time to digest this news."

Jason saw that Jade wasn't convinced a new contract could be attained and seemed to fear what he might say next. The woebegone expression on her face squeezed at his heartstrings. He didn't want to hurt the woman he loved. He only wanted to reassure her that she didn't have to fear the future and should be excited about this opportunity, but when she glanced his way, her expression appeared guarded. Fear marred her beautiful face. He pulled her into his arms, aware of her quivering breath. Was he wrong about this appointment? Had he made a mistake by contacting her former agent?

"Jade, don't let fear ruin an opportunity to win your future."

"I don't know. There's a lot to consider."

"Like what?"

"Like my health, and my addiction. My music career was partially responsible for my unhealthy choices. I'm not sure I want to take the risk."

"I think you do."

She stared at him fixedly. "Why are you so sure of your position?" she said, her tone sharp.

"I know what I hear. I listen to you sing; I watch you strumming your guitar, and I know you've been writing new songs. Even if you were never to tour again, you could still market your music, maybe regain the income you want. Dixon could support your future goals."

"Have you told him… I've been writing?"

"Yes, I have." Jason winked, nudging her on the arm. "I might have mentioned there's a few love songs in the mix, too, inspired by yours truly."

She shook her head, the first hint of a smile brightened her expression. "You're full of surprises, Mr. Knight."

"Hey, I see you're not pleased, but I'd do anything to see you smile. To see you happy."

"I am happy." She reached forward and grasped his grizzled cheek. "I should be angry with you for contacting Dixon without talking to me first, but I don't have the willpower to be angry. It means so much to me that you would support me. Make me happier still. Kiss me."

He held back. "Will you go?"

Jason watched Jade while she processed his question. The silence stretched for several seconds.

"You know what, yes, I will. When do we leave?"

"Tomorrow."

"Tomorrow? Jason… The highway is closed!"

"It'll be open by the time morning arrives. I booked our flight two weeks ago, but I couldn't bring myself to tell you."

Jade shook her head, bit at her lip. Her facial expression took on a whole new tone of white. "I don't know what to say. This is sudden and a lot for me to take in. You're crazy, Jason. I'm scared out of my mind, but I love you *more than ever* for believing in me."

He pulled her closer still, embracing her, giving her a quick peck on the lips. "Hey, I'll do anything for you. I'll stand beside you for the rest of my life. I'm crazy in love with you!"

"I'll need more than love to get through this meeting."

"Whatever you need, I'll make sure you have it. You're not alone. Sweetheart, I'm not only trying to help you, I'm also supporting your future goals. I understand the trauma you've suffered. I just want you to know, we're in this fight together."

Jade seemed emotional. Tears formed in her eyes. She

grasped his hand and held on tight. "Thank you," she murmured, her voice quivering. "I don't know how I'll ever repay your kindness."

He pulled her into his embrace and massaged her lower back. "No worries, sweetheart. I promise you, it will be okay. Go back to your book. Read, take your mind off the meeting, until Monday comes."

CHAPTER 22

"Jade Carter," The Agency's receptionist exclaimed, "it's good to see you. You look amazing."

Standing in the reception area, Jade inhaled deeply, trying to dispel her worries. She scrutinized Jason's supportive expression and then regarded an acquaintance she hadn't seen in months. Though Patsy was smiling and appeared friendly, Jade didn't speak for several seconds. She tried to build her self-confidence, knowing she had entered a place where she had suffered a severe trauma. Maybe an earthquake was occurring because it seemed like the office tower was swaying, either that or she was the one shuddering.

If Patsy noticed her discomfort, she displayed no outward signs. In fact, she rushed from her workspace, hurrying around the counter, soon reaching for her hands and holding them within her grip. A huge smile lit her face.

Jade didn't know what to say. *When had she grown so shy, so weak?*

"It's good to see you. Just look at you—" Patsy breathed, observing her winter-white pant suit. "It brings joy to my heart to see you dressed so well and appearing so healthy. Look at your face, your smooth complexion, and perfectly applied make up. Why, your eyes are sparkling like diamonds."

"It's kind of you to say, Patsy." Jade took a deep breath, scrutinizing the office space. "I see nothing much has changed around here."

"Something's changed, our star is back! Our singer has made a transformation. You have a new light in your eyes."

"It's love," Jason interjected, "love does wonders for a woman."

"Patsy, permit me to introduce Jason Knight, my fiancé."

"Your fiancé? Please accept my heartfelt congratulations. I'm glad life has been good to you, but I won't keep you waiting. I'll let Dixon know you're here. He's been looking forward to seeing you."

"Has he?"

Patsy grabbed her wrist. "Jade Carter, it's not like you to be so timid. Everything will be okay. You know that, right?"

Despite the welcome, Jade took a deep breath. "I suppose I'll find out soon enough."

Alone, Jade left the reception area and walked toward Dixon's office, her stomach churning with nervous tension. The corridor, though short, seemed miles long. Gathering her courage, she placed one foot in front of the other and progressed toward her future. *I can do this.*

She paused beside a wall of glassed-in cubicles and stood next to the glass, studying agents at their work. Unsmiling, a woman peered in her direction. No matter how much time passed, Jade knew she'd never escape the shame of her addictions. She lowered her head, glancing away, and proceeded toward the office at the end of the corridor.

Dixon's door was open, so she peeked inside his office. Taking a deep breath, she stole inside like a thief in the night, glancing nervously at her former agent where he sat at his desk.

He must have heard her approaching as he turned to her and smiled, but his expression couldn't be described as one of happiness, more of curiosity.

"Welcome back, Jade. Please, take a seat."

She took a deep breath, then walked across the brief space and sat. "Same office, same white leather chairs. I'd have thought you would have replaced them by now."

"Yes, well, with declining budgets and the loss of prized clients, I have to make do. You look good by the way. How have you been?"

Jade studied Dixon's face, avoiding his question. He watched her, too, scrutinizing her expression. His perusal made her more uncomfortable. She took a deep breath. Hedged. "I've never been better."

"Is that so? Your hands are shaking, Jade."

She lifted her hand and studied her fingers. "This? This is anxiety. Nerves, Dixon." She squeezed her hand. "But I understand why you would think otherwise."

"Let's cut to the chase. You look good. Your skin glows with supposed health, your eyes are bright, you're as beautiful as ever, and…"

"And what?"

"And for the first time in month's, you're on time for a meeting."

Jade shook her head. "That has nothing to do with my health or my addiction. Jason made sure I was on time."

"Your new flame?"

"My fiancé deserves some respect. He's been good to me."

"Once we've completed our conversation, I'd like to meet the man. We've talked on the phone and he's been a strong advocate for you, but if what he says is true and you have recovered, I'd like to thank him in person."

"I'd like you to meet him, but you should know from the onset of this discussion that I'm not recovered." Jade glanced at her fingers, massaging the tips, searching for inner strength. "Dixon, my name is Jade Carter and I'm an alcoholic. As you know, I have issues with certain drugs, too. After you released me from my contract, I travelled to the town of Harmony. While I was there, I made a bad decision. I'm sure you've heard about it. The ugly truth was published in the papers."

"I'm aware of the story."

"After I was released from hospital, I entered an outpatient treatment program in Harmony, a program that has supported my recovery and continued abstinence from addictive substances. I have not had a drink in six months."

"Why are you telling me this? It's not what I thought you'd say."

"Dixon— I want my career back, but in such a way that I can live a healthy, normal, and meaningful life. I never want to use again."

"Your fingers are not shaking anymore."

Jade swallowed. "Nerves, Dixon."

He leaned backward in his chair. "You don't have to be nervous; not with me. I only ever wanted the best for you."

"I appreciate that."

"Your champion and fiancé, Jason, tells me you've been writing songs. How's that going?"

Jade smiled for the first time. "It's amazing. I never thought I could write without Taylor, but there's something about the beauty of a mountain town that inspires lyrics. I sit in the cabin, staring at the mountains, and the words just come to me."

"All love songs?" Dixon asked, his eyebrows rising in amusement.

"Hey, a girl who's in love writes love songs," Jade giggled, relaxing.

"Okay, so let's get back to the reason for this meeting. Jade, what do you want from me, from the Agency?"

She didn't hesitate. Jade decided to lay her heart on the line. "I want my career back. I want to make a new promise to my fans and the Agency, that I'll never disappoint you or my audience again." Dixon placed his elbows on his desk and he clasped his fingers together, then laid his chin on them. "What's the matter, Dixon?"

He suddenly appeared emotional. Jade had never witnessed any form of sentiment from her agent before. He appeared as if he might…

"I thought I'd never see you again." He shook his head.

"I know what you thought," Jade lamented, sighing. "Let's not go there. I can't change the past, but I can change my future. Let's talk about the future."

Patsy knocked on the door. "What is it, Patsy?"

"Have you given Jade the contract yet?"

"We're getting there."

Patsy trudged into the office and passed Dixon a contract and Jade a pen. "Enough small talk. This singer is as nervous as a child without its mother. What more do you need to know?"

Suddenly, Jason was at the door, too. "Sorry, I stayed in the reception area for as long as I could. I know it's not professional to intrude on your business discussion, but I had to know what's happening, too."

Jade smiled. Sweet harmony, she loved this man.

Dixon cleared his throat. "Jade, we'd like to offer you a new contract."

Tears welled in her eyes. "I can't believe it. I never expected this would happen." She glanced at Jason, knowing she wouldn't be here without his business acumen. "Where do I sign?"

"On the dotted line, Jade Carter, just like the first time," Patsy prompted, pointing.

Jade paused, holding the pen. "Wait a minute. Before I do this, you need to know that I'm not leaving the town of Harmony. My support system is there. My work will have to be done from the town."

"You write the songs and we'll help you lay down the tracks."

"I have a surprise for you," Jason said, grinning. "The town council has approved a new building in Harmony. You'll love it. The Harmony Music Centre, which will include a concert hall and a recording studio."

"So you see," Dixon said, giving Jason a conspiratorial wink, "you'll have a place to write your songs, lay down new tracks, sing, entertain an audience, and support the community you have come to love."

"This comes as a big surprise. I don't know what to say."

"Say thank you, country star," Patsy coaxed, winking. "And once you've signed the papers, we'll celebrate with a glass of club soda."

"Thank you," Jade said, taking a deep breath. "I feel like I have everything I've ever wanted and more." Grateful, she stared at Jason's joyous expression. The man was clearly happy and supportive of her interests. She reached for his hand and held it firmly, squeezing his fingers. She wouldn't be here without him.

Dixon rose from his office chair and walked around his desk, soon reaching for her free hand. Jade released Jason's grasp and accepted Dixon's handshake. "Congratulations, Jade, welcome back to the Agency."

Jade's visit with her mother had earned her a headache. She massaged her forehead, remembering the conversation and their past. Given this was their first visit in over two years, she couldn't assume that a mother daughter relationship would be as strong as when times were good. Some moments had been difficult; she'd apologized for past transgressions, becoming emotional, and subsequently they had both cried tears of regret, but if there were positives to come from their discussion, at least they were talking now. Time seemed to heal all wounds. Jade hoped that was true.

She thanked Jason for forcing her to see her mother. This step not only assisted with mending old wounds, but also aided in her recovery, assisting her to climb another life hurdle.

After the visit, Jason and Jade had departed for Vancouver International airport. The return flight to Calgary had passed smoothly with little turbulence. Jade could have sat in the First Class Cabin, but had insisted on the economy section.

A few passengers had openly stared at her as she'd

maneuvered along the aisle of the airplane. She hadn't retreated from guests who had made eye contact. In fact, she had smiled at a few passengers, no longer embarrassed by her past.

Flying over the mountains, she'd had time to reflect on her future goals. *What did she want from life? What songs would she write next? What were her goals for the future?* Jade Carter knew she had a second chance at life and she didn't need to win the world overnight.

Living a healthy and happier life with the man she loved, *one day at a time,* was her new motto.

THANK you for reading *A Lasting Harmony.* If you enjoyed Jason and Jade's love story, your honest opinion of their romance will support the author's writing career. Please rate or review this book on your favorite book site, review site, blog, or your own social media properties, and share your opinion with other readers. Thank you!

THE THURSTON HOTEL SERIES

A Thurston Promise, Brenda Sinclair

Opposite of Frozen, Jan O'Hara

Love Under Construction, Sheila Seabrook

A Lasting Harmony, Shelley Kassian

With Open Arms, M. K. Stelmack

The Starlight Garden, Maeve Buchanan

The Thurston Heirloom, Suzanne Stengl

An Angel's Secret, Ellen Jorgy

To a Tea, Katie O'Connor

A Thurston Christmas, Brenda Sinclair

CONTACT SHELLEY KASSIAN

If you would like to learn more about Shelley or her novels, visit her website at shelleykassian.com. Here you can read excerpts from her books, linked reviews, blog posts, as well as discovering her professional affiliations and accreditation.

Shelley enjoys hearing from her readers. If you'd like to contact the author, send her a message at: shelleykassian@gmail.com.

FOLLOW SHELLEY ON SOCIAL MEDIA

amazon.com/author/shelleykassian

bookbub.com/authors/shelley-kassian

goodreads.com/shelleykassian

facebook.com/ShelleyKassian

instagram.com/shelleykassian

twitter.com/@shelleykassian

pinterest.com/shelleykassian

ABOUT SHELLEY KASSIAN

Bestselling author Shelley Kassian has been writing timeless love stories filled with romance or dark fantasy (romantasy) for more than twenty years, novels that include her recent true love story, *A Mountain Leads Home*. A history enthusiast, she's traveled far and wide to explore secret gardens and medieval castles, having an avid interest in the Tudor period. Her prose has been described as "near rhapsodic," "pitch perfect," and "stylishly straightforward, rarely relying on complex turns of phrase." Reviewers have said her narrative conveys "imaginative fantasy," "fascinating characters," and "refreshing romance."

Shelley's taken creative writing courses, holds board positions within professional associations, and retains a Professional Editing Certificate. Drawing on her expertise, she has mentored novice writers, but her passion comes alive while scribing her stories into novel-length fiction. Shelley shares her life with her husband, adores her adult children and two grand pups, and when not relaxing at her seaside cottage, lives in Calgary, Alberta, Canada.